A SCOT OF HER OWN

Once Upon a Scot Series
Book One

by Maeve Greyson

ARE YOU SIGNED UP FOR DRAGONBLADE'S BLOG?

You'll get the latest news and information on exclusive giveaways, exclusive excerpts, coming releases, sales, free books, cover reveals and more.

Check out our complete list of authors, too!

No spam, no junk. That's a promise!

Sign Up Here

www.dragonbladepublishing.com

Dearest Reader;

Thank you for your support of a small press. At Dragonblade Publishing, we strive to bring you the highest quality Historical Romance from some of the best authors in the business. Without your support, there is no 'us', so we sincerely hope you adore these stories and find some new favorite authors along the way.

Happy Reading!

CEO, Dragonblade Publishing

Additional Dragonblade books by Author Maeve Greyson

Once Upon a Scot Series
A Scot of Her Own

Time to Love a Highlander Series
Loving Her Highland Thief
Taming Her Highland Legend
Winning Her Highland Warrior

Highland Heroes Series
The Guardian
The Warrior
The Judge
The Dreamer
The Bard
The Ghost

CHAPTER ONE

Isle of Mull, Scotland
July 1273

"**S**EVEN FECKIN' YEARS since the treaty. Do they live for nothing but battle?"

"As we do?" Thorburn MacDougall shot a warning glare at his brother. Ross knew better than to natter on like a spoiled bairn while tracking the enemy. With a hard shove of his shield, he pointed them all toward the last known location of the rebellious Northmen.

"We are different from them," Ross argued in a good-natured whisper. "A silver groat a day leases my battle axe for any wee skirmishes needed. 'Tis an occupation. No' an obsession."

Valan, youngest of the three MacDougall brothers, snorted. "A silver groat and all the wenches ye can bed, aye?"

"Enough!" Thorburn strained to keep his voice down. "I will have quiet, or it's the whipping post for both of ye, ye ken?" He doled out another quelling look to ensure they understood he meant it. As constable of the Lord of Argyll's *Gallóglaigh* warriors, he maintained the strictest discipline and did not exclude kin. If these two foiled this campaign, he'd order them whipped until they begged forgiveness for their lack of self-control.

Although he commanded hundreds, only a few of his best crept alongside him into the edge of the forest. Six warriors, including himself and his brothers. All assisted by their weaponry knaves. Spies had reported the rogue Norwegians numbered at naught but two and twenty. Six mighty *Gallóglaigh* could easily best that few. The last band of rebels had been well over a hundred, infesting the northeastern woodlands of Mull like lice on a priest. Twoscore of his men had ousted that lot with little effort. Attacked and made it back to Duart in time to enjoy a celebratory feast after a mere four days.

A familiar whooshing warned of incoming arrows.

"Shields!" Thorburn bellowed, shoving his upward.

He hated shields. Now, sword, axe, spear, and arrow? Aye, those were fine weapons indeed. Not a bloody shield to cower behind. But the last time they met with King Magnus's traitors, archers in the trees had been an unavoidable annoyance, so shields it was. Without taking his focus off the trees up ahead, he reached behind him. "Spear!"

The shaft of the weapon smacked into his outstretched hand as if placed there by some mystical force. He hurled it with a guttural roar, then gave a satisfied jerk of his chin. His target cried out and tumbled from its perch high in the branches.

"The first of many," his weaponry knave called out. Tasgall enjoyed keeping tally, and Thorburn didn't mind. At least it taught the lad his numbers.

Another volley of arrows followed. An artful shot caught him in the shoulder, piercing through the mesh of his hauberk. He snapped off the shaft and threw it aside. Hendry, his provision knave, would remove the rest later. The haft of his sword slapped into his palm without his even asking. Tasgall knew his preference in weapons.

"End this!" Thorburn ordered, then unleashed a bloodcurdling war cry signaling a full-on charge.

Shields raised, they rushed the trees to flush the archers from their roosts. Thorburn stormed deeper into the woods. Bowmen were always the first line. He wanted the rest, those waiting to battle hand to hand.

A lone Northman stepped into his path.

Thorburn unleashed a loud, rumbling laugh. This wouldn't take long.

Slight of build and a full head shorter, his opponent appeared less than fearsome. But then the man sprang forward, swinging both axe and sword with enough agility and skill to make up for his diminutive stature.

The longer Thorburn parried and fought the irritating churl, the less amused he became. Every move, every thrust, the agile Northman countered it, adjusted defense, then skittered out of reach like a leaf riding the wind. It was as though the fiend enshrouded in that strange bascinet knew his every move before he took it. Eyes glittering like ice, the man made naught a sound. Not even a grunt. His helm's elaborate visor and camail hid his features. It was like fighting a faceless wraith that darted in and out among the trees like a vengeful spirit of the wood.

An upward swipe of his foe's blade nicked Thorburn's chin. The sting of the cut yanked him free of the demon's bemusing spell, scolding him like a mother's slap. He would nay let his mind wander again. 'Twas becoming more than a little obvious that his hulking size hindered more than helped in this tight forest terrain. A tactical error on his part. He had also allowed a vainglorious attitude to trick him into underestimating this opponent. Such an error in judgment would not happen again.

A felled tree, small and partially hidden by vines, caught his eye and prompted a plan. He veered to the left, matching the sidestep with a mighty swing of his sword. A calculated swipe. Not meant to maim or injure but herd his adversary into a trap. Nay, he would not end this fiend just yet. Instead, he would topple the unsuspecting fool and rip off his helm before delivering the killing blow. He hungered to see fear etched on this man's face. Yearned to watch the terrifying knowledge of impending death replace the calculating ice in the Northman's clear blue eyes.

Again, the devil thwarted his plan, leaping across the obstacle with the agility of a deer.

Thorburn longed to roar out his rage, but he would not give the lout that satisfaction. Nay, he knew better than to let emotions lead him into foolhardy moves. But he would allow his fury to fuel a charge into the clearing up ahead. Time to take the safety of the trees away from this insolent wretch.

The small warrior did his best to avoid the open area, but Thorburn wouldn't allow it. The forest had thinned enough to do what he loved best. Rid himself of that accursed shield. With a rapid-fire punching throw, he hurled the weighty disk of metal and wood. It hit the Northman with enough force to launch him well into the clearing. The wee demon landed hard, flat of his back, right where Thorburn wanted him. Now he allowed himself a victorious roar as he thundered forward to claim his prey.

An impressive crease in the metal chest plate attached to his opponent's chain mail revealed where the shield had hit. The sound of strained wheezing behind the man's visor confirmed it.

"Allow me to end yer misery for ye." Thorburn unsheathed his dagger, planted a knee on the devil's heaving chest, then ripped off the man's helm and froze.

"Well?" The captivating woman made a defiant upward jerk of her chin. "Do it!" The frost in her icy blue eyes had disappeared. Fury and fire flashed like lightning in their depths. "Do it, *feiging!*"

Mouth ajar, he stared down at her, then dragged his gaze from her snarling countenance all the way to her boot tips. Beneath all that leather padding, chain mail, and strategically placed armor plating was a woman. And a beautiful woman at that. "Are yer men so incapable of fighting in yer stead?"

She spit in his face, then bared her teeth, showing them even and white as pearls. "Either kill me or let me go. I have no time for dullard Scots."

Thorburn swiped the spittle away, then eased up on the pressure of his knee on her chest but didn't remove it completely. She might be a woman, but she had already proven herself an adversary to be taken seriously. "More of ye were spotted than these few here in this wood. Where are the rest?" Another troubling thought occurred. "And are all of them lasses?"

A stony glare was her only response.

Even though he figured it futile, he nudged the tip of his dagger up under her chin. Such a long slender, soft-looking throat she had. A tender place made for a man's kisses, not the blade of a weapon. "What is yer name, my vicious wee minx?"

She worked her jaws as though about to spit again, so he clapped a hand over her mouth. "Every time ye spit, I shall order yer rations cut until yer mouth goes so dry yer tongue shrivels, ye ken?"

Her eyes narrowed into slits of simmering hatred.

Still holding her mouth so she couldn't bite or spit, Thorburn frowned down at this tempting dilemma under his knee. By all rights, he should kill her. It had never been his nature to take prisoners. They only wasted precious resources. Guards. Food. Time. And one such as her would be an irksome distraction among his men until they either took her with them when they returned to Argyll or sent her back to King Magnus in Norway to punish for breaking the Treaty of Perth.

But he couldn't bring himself to kill her. Not a woman. She might fight like a man, but she was still a lass.

Frustration and something akin to embarrassment at his own soft-heartedness filled him. Commander to scores of warriors. Known as ruthless, unrelenting, and cold. Not once had he ever hurt a woman or child. It wasn't in him, nor in his brothers. He also never allowed it among the ranks of his men. They had nailed the last man who disobeyed this standing order to a post on the tiny Isle of Muck and left him there. He did not tolerate disobedience among his *Gallóglaigh,* and they knew it. In that matter, his heart was hard as stone.

"Forgive me, m'lord," Tasgall called out. "I didna mean to lag. Feckers snared me in a pit deep enough for a pair of boars."

The beauty twitched beneath him. One of her pale brows

arched higher, and amusement sparkled in her eyes. The knave's announcement pleased her.

"Wily as well as wicked, are ye? Well done then." Thorburn eased away his hand and knee but flipped the lass and twisted her wrists behind her back. "Bindings," he ordered, holding out his hand without pulling his gaze from the intricate braids tied in place around the lass's head. No wonder she hadn't worn a padded coif beneath her helm. The thickness of that lustrous hair protected her better than any quilting.

"A woman," Tasgall said in a hushed tone as he came to a stumbling stop.

"Aye." Thorburn frowned up at the gangly lad who rarely suffered from such ineptness. "Bindings?" he repeated with a snap of his fingers.

"Forgive me." The boy hurried to offer the length of braided leather he'd pulled from the sack slung over his shoulder. "Do ye mean to keep her, then? As prisoner?"

Thorburn knew exactly what Tasgall was thinking and couldn't care less. However, the *Gallóglaigh* knaves gossiped and twisted the details of the warriors they served into such grand lies that a kernel of truth couldn't be found. They each wished to outdo the other. Tasgall and Hendry's mutterings held extra weight because they served him. This situation demanded careful handling.

"I will keep her 'til I see fit to do otherwise," he said as he rose to his feet and forced the lovely, armored lady to hers. He tipped his head toward the trees. "Fetch my shield. Then ye'll be holding this one's lead."

"Aye, m'lord." The lad loped away.

"And ye will nay give him any trouble, or there'll be no food or water for ye, ye ken?" He caught one of her fallen braids between his fingers. Silky and pale as fresh cream poured from a pitcher. He had never seen hair so white on a woman. When she failed to acknowledge she had heard what he said, he tugged on the braid. "No trouble from ye, understand?"

The gossamer-haired fury spun and caught the side of his knee with the back of her heel.

Excruciating pain doubled him, but he latched hold of her and shoved her back to the ground. As he held her fast, he ran a hand down to his throbbing knee. A warm wetness met his touch, blood already soaked his trews. He grabbed hold of her foot and lifted it. The wily cat had spikes fitted to the back of her boots.

"Replace those boots with shackles," he ordered, grunting as he struggled to stand and plant a foot on her back to keep her still.

"I dinna tote shackles, m'lord." Tasgall dropped to his knees and frantically rooted through his leather sack. "Forgive me, but ye never take prisoners." His muffled apology came from deep within the bag. The lad had nearly crawled fully inside it. He emerged with a length of rope in one hand and a replacement chain for Thorburn's heavy mace. "I can fashion one with these."

"Then do it."

The lady twisted, glared up at him, then spit again. The vixen had deadly aim and amazing range.

He swiped the back of his hand across his forehead. "And gag her!"

Gagged. Barefoot. Shackled and bound to the knobby end of a spear pole manned by Tasgall, their enraged prisoner led the march back through the woods.

"Keep tight hold of that stick, boy. Dinna underestimate her." Thorburn limped along behind them, wondering what kind of poison the wicked temptress had used to coat her boot spikes. The puncture she had dealt him hurt worse than the time he had caught a mace in the knee. That wound had crippled him for weeks, but at least he had never lost the feeling in his toes. His foot had gone so numb, he struggled to walk without stumbling.

Maybe old Marta could get it out of her. A healer from one of the villages on Mull, Marta was of Norse descent, too. But one who had no issue paying allegiance to a Scottish king rather than one from Norway.

Tasgall looked proud to oversee their captive. Poor lad. Slight of body and cunning as could be, the smaller-than-normal boy would never make a warrior. But he was courageous, attentive, and good with both bow and spear. For that, he kept his position as weaponry knave to the commander. And now as guard to their lovely yet infuriating wee hellcat.

Ross appeared, wearing the foolish grin that signaled the end of a successful battle. "A prisoner? What do ye mean to do with a..." His brother's voice trailed off, and his head slowly tilted, reminding Thorburn of one of the Lord of Argyll's dogs.

"She is my spoil of war." Thorburn clapped a hand atop Tasgall's shoulder, bringing both the lad and woman to a bouncing stop.

"Spoil of war?" Ross repeated. His head tilted to the other side, and his lopsided grin grew. "Since when do ye *indulge* in spoils of war, brother?"

"Since I am constable and decide to do so." Thorburn pulled a spear from Tasgall's harness and used it as a staff to lean on. He limped closer to the bodies laid out just beyond the edge of the woods. All Northmen. No losses of their own. Good. "How many?"

"There's naught but ten here. I thought Edrid reported four and twenty?" Valan stepped away from the others, still rifling through the belongings of the lifeless warriors. "None fled. All stood their ground and fought."

"There is eleven," Ross interrupted with a grin. "Thor's got himself a pet."

"A pet?" Valan repeated, then came up short as he caught sight of the captive. "A woman?"

"A spoil of war," Thorburn corrected, then fixed a dogged look at the rolling hillside unfurling in front of him. It would be a long walk back to camp. A long, painful walk. Thank goodness they had horses to get them back to the coast and Duart. Even though the new castle wasn't yet complete, it was livable and served as a decent home away from home until they returned to Argyll. But they would spend tonight and possibly longer in camp. They needed to find the remaining Northmen and deal with them before returning to Duart.

"And where will ye keep this wee distraction of yers?" Ross asked as he fell in step beside him.

"In my tent," he said without hesitation, daring his brother to make a comment that would land him on his arse. "Send Tam or Niall to fetch the healer. I am none too sure Hendry can deal with this poison."

"Poison?" Valan eyed him up and down as he took his place on Thor's left. "Ye dinna look poisoned. Mad as hell, but nay poisoned." He grabbed hold of Thorburn's shoulder and peered at what was left of the arrow that had pierced his chain mail. "It's naught but a wee arrow. Hendry's sewed up worse than that before."

"The leg wound, aye?" He was in no mood for either of his brothers' chatter. Getting back to camp was his current priority. That, and getting to know the spitting banshee better. Not only would she be able to provide them information regarding the rest of the traitors, but he had never been one to shirk from the challenge of charming a beautiful woman.

"Shall I tote ye on my back?" Ross asked with an evil smirk.

"I suggest both of ye fall back and hold yer tongues before I assign ye to shoveling horse shite with the knaves, ye ken?"

His brothers took the hint and left him alone, walking far enough behind to grant him a bit of quiet for contemplation. He ignored their occasional snickers. After all, he couldn't kill them. If he did, he would have no family at all. To save his siblings from a good thrashing, he focused on the intriguing puzzle in front of him. Even walking at the end of a pole, she held her shoulders back and fisted her bound hands at the small of her back. An air of authority added to the beguiling mystery surrounding this fine warrior princess. This lass was someone important. Or if she wasn't, she should be. "Slow her, Tasgall."

Thorburn limped up beside her, studying the fearless woman who would as soon kill him as to look at him. The lady held her head high and stared straight ahead, never flinching as she shuffled through the grass barefooted. The land might be lush and green this far into summer, but rocks and sharp dried grasses from the season's past hid across the verdant hillside. She never stumbled or reacted. With her spirit, he had no doubt she would dance across beds of hot coals with a smile.

She even managed to stomp while wearing the makeshift shackles. Like an infuriated queen. Expressionless. Cold. Probably plotting her escape as well as his murder with every step she took. What a delightful prize the day had gifted him. He had not been this intrigued about anything in a very long while.

"Never ye fear, m'lady," he said as if they strolled arm in arm through a garden. "We willna leave yer countryman to the scavengers. A runner will be sent to the nearest village. The people will fetch them and see them sent back to wherever the lot of ye came from."

She didn't twitch. Just marched onward.

"Are ye from here on Mull?" he asked. Even gagged, she could answer a yay or nay question. If she would.

She granted him a bored roll of her eyes, filling him with a sense of victory at achieving the reaction.

"So, ye are like the others then? In from Norway, to plague the building of Duart and stir trouble amongst the villagers." He gimped along like an old sage, leaning heavily on the shaft of the spear. "Ye waste yer time and lives doing such." With a shrug, he tossed his free hand in the air. "If ye wish to live here, live here. What does it matter that ye're now under Scottish rule? Haakon was a greedy man. Like most kings, I suppose. His son appears to have a bit more sense." Another sharp pain shot through his knee and down his leg, making him wonder if she had somehow ordered it. He stifled a groan, determined to keep the one-sided conversation going. "I'm sure Magnus is just as greedy as his father, but instead of fighting to keep the land, he bartered it for a fair amount of silver. Shrewd, if ye ask me, and I am a man who lives for warring." He gave her a wink. "But I'm mighty fond of silver as well."

She pulled in a deep breath and huffed it out, her delicate nostrils flaring.

"So, I'm boring ye, am I?"

That won him another roll of her eyes.

"Once we reach camp, ye will be settled in my quarters. Given water and food." With a stern arch of a brow, he added, "As long as ye dinna continue with yer infernal spitting, aye?"

He thought she twitched a shoulder but couldn't be certain. All he knew for sure was that the muscles in her jaw flexed, then tightened as she resettled her bite into the leather gag. When her eyes narrowed, he knew something was about to happen.

She lunged backward, ramming the pole into Tasgall's gut and ripping it free of his hands. Then she spun and twisted, hit it on a rise in the ground, and dislodged the thing from the knot at her wrists.

Thorburn knocked her into the dirt. "Stop! Have ye no sense at all?"

Her glare seared him, fully communicating the depths of her hatred.

"Aye, well, since ye already hate me, m'lady, 'tis about to get worse." He turned to the still gasping Tasgall. "Cut off her armor. I want her left in nothing but her léine and trews." He gave a satisfied nod. "And check all her bindings to ensure they're still well knotted."

"Yes, m'lord." Tasgall dug in his sack in search of the shears he used to repair Thorburn's hauberk. "Will she not be faster then, m'lord? Lighter on her feet to run?"

"Nay," Thorburn said, his glare still locked with hers. "She willna be on her feet but over my shoulder like a sack of grain."

"Ye are wounded, brother. Yer shoulder. Knee." Ross smiled down at the fierce maiden. "I would be happy to tote yer pet for ye."

"Nay." Thorburn stood taller, energized by the challenge. If it was a battle this wee vixen wanted, then a battle she would have.

"I will have no problem carrying this one."

It took Tasgall a bit of time to cut through the chain mail and strip it away. "'Tis a pity to ruin such workmanship," he commented while peeling off the strips of woven metal and plates engraved with elaborate knots and whorls. Upon reaching a layer of leather covering another layer of padding, he looked up at Thorburn. "All of it but her tunic, aye?"

"Aye." Thorburn supervised with his arms folded across his chest.

"What if she doesna wear a léine?"

Thorburn sensed dangerous ground here. His code still stood. No harm or humiliation to women or children. What he did with this one could very well undermine his longstanding policy. Even claiming her as a spoil of war risked making him look a hypocrite. Order and respect must be maintained above all else. "If ye dinna see the hem of a tunic, leave her covered with that innermost haubergeon of cloth."

After a disappointed tip of his head, Tasgall bent to the task.

Stripped of her battle shell, the sparring hen was now a quarter of her original size. No wonder he had thought her male. Even now, clothed in nothing but her linen tunic and dark trews, whatever curves she had were still well concealed by the oversized shirt that reached almost to her knees.

He pulled her to her feet, then bent and threw her over his uninjured shoulder. Still gagged and with her hands tied behind her back, her ladyship could do little else but hang there and ride. Or so he thought. Once again, the wily minx impressed him with her ability to adapt to anything he did. Within sight of camp, a warm wetness flooded his shoulder and spread down his chest. The conniving wench had gifted him with a healthy soaking of piss.

With a determined snort, he shifted his hold and continued walking. "Ross says some men pay extra for that in the brothels." Perhaps he should have left her lashed to a tree. It would have been a hell of a lot less trouble. Although, her warm softness bouncing against his cheek wasn't entirely unpleasant. And through the scent of sweat and piss, her unmistakable womanly musk worked its magic, reminding him that a lovely maid hadn't warmed his bed in several long weeks. But now, weary and sore as he was, he doubted very much if he possessed the energy or patience to attempt a seduction of this spiteful wee hedgehog.

With all eyes locked on him, he limped into camp with his prize over his shoulder. When he reached his tent, he dumped her to the ground. "Proper shackles on her wrists and ankles," he ordered, handing the spear he had used as a crutch back to Tasgall. "Then stake her. Inside my tent. To the back wall, ye ken? Ye've seen how she is. If she escapes, it's yer arse."

"She willna escape, m'lord," Tasgall swore with certainty. "I grant ye that."

"Ale, m'lord?" Hendry offered a welcomed tankard that Thorburn drained, then held out for another.

"I've an arrow for ye to dig out, Hendry, but a healer's been called for the knee."

The ruddy-haired lad, short and plump as a partridge, wrinkled his freckled nose. "Got water set to boiling and ready. A fine broth, some roasted meat, and fried bread as well, m'lord."

"Ye're a good lad, Hendry. Just more ale, a good wash, and a change of clothes for now." Thorburn limped into his large tent, as furnished and comfortable as any private room in a keep. As constable of the *Gallóglaigh*, he expected nothing less.

"I'll set more water on the fire, m'lord," Hendry assured, then rushed away to put all requests in motion.

The rattle of chains and ringing ping of a hammer hitting iron drew Thorburn's attention to the far side of the tent. Tasgall had worked quickly. Their guest sat with her back against a heavy trunk. Her shackled hands were now in front of her with her arms looped around the one knee she could bend to her chest because of the length of the chain between the shackles on her ankles.

"Leave her gagged, m'lord?" Tasgall asked as he finished driving a second iron stake through another ring in the chain beside her left ankle.

"Aye. For now." He wasn't in the mood to be spit at again and, at this point, wouldn't be surprised if the wench breathed fire. "Two stakes?"

"Aye, m'lord." The lad gave a serious nod. "I'll no' be risking yer ire 'cause of her escaping."

"Good lad." Thorburn gimped across the furs spread inside the tent. "Strip me down so Hendry can see to the arrow. I dinna ken how badly it damaged the mesh."

"Aye, m'lord." Tasgall untucked the extra length of Thorburn's long leather belt, then unbuckled it. He frowned down at the stained leather as he hugged the sheathed sword and dagger attached to the belt under one arm. "This is wet, m'lord."

"Our guest christened me with piss." Thorburn tossed his helm and dagger atop the trunk Tasgall used for cleaning and repairs. "My hauberk will want a good oiling once ye've cleaned and repaired it." After a glance at his scowling prisoner, he added, "I'm sure Lady Viper's piss corrodes like acid."

"More ale for ye, m'lord." Hendry held out a tankard while casting a side-eyed glance at the woman. "And what about her, m'lord?"

"What about her?"

"Be she allowed food and drink?"

"Not yet," Thorburn said. "If she behaves for a bit, maybe then. For now, bring the basin and jar. I'm due a good scrubbing." He lowered himself to a stool, so his boots could be removed. After another glance at his surly prize, he grinned. He would convince the lovely lady to remember her manners. "But bring in my supper first and set it on a table just out of her reach, aye? I wish for her to enjoy the aroma of yer fine cooking."

Her narrow-eyed glower filled him with hollow victory. This could be so much more pleasant if only she would allow it. Ties undone, the front of her tunic sagged open, revealing a mouth-watering expanse of pale skin and the teasing swell of one breast. He allowed his gaze to linger. Aye, it could be so much more pleasant.

She yanked the neckline shut and balled up even more, turning away from him as much as the chain allowed.

As Hendry lit additional candles, Thorburn frowned. The fawn color of the pelt beneath her was stained with blood. Either the woman suffered from her monthly courses, or she was wounded. A wound he could manage. Courses? Nay. That was women's magic and dangerous sorcery. Known to bring ill luck to men by the power granted females during that time.

"Hendry." He tipped his head toward the lass. "See to her, aye?"

"See to her, m'lord?" the boy repeated with a leery widening of his eyes.

"Aye." Thorburn pointed at the pelt. "There's blood there. I dinna think I wounded her, but…"

Usually obedient, Hendry balked and stared at him as though he thought him mad.

Thorburn arched a brow. Knaves never disobeyed. "If she is wounded, she must be tended to." He didn't voice the other possibility, but judging by the redness of the lad's face, Hendry had already thought of it.

The boy opened his mouth to speak, then closed it. He stared at the bloody pelt as though the thing might attack at any moment.

A rustling at the front of the tent made Thorburn turn. "Marta. 'Tis glad I am to see ye."

"Thank God in Heaven above," Hendry said with a relieved breath that nearly blew out three of the candles. He crossed himself and backed away, edging toward the door. "I'll be bringing in the supper now, m'lord, and the hot water for Mistress Marta."

The older woman, wizened and small as dried fruit from seasons past, came up short at the sight of the prisoner. "A woman, Constable? In chains?" Accusation and disgust dripped from her every word.

He would ignore it for now. "See to her first," he ordered. "She bleeds."

CHAPTER TWO

ADELLIS BJØRNSDÓTTIR RECOGNIZED the healer and couldn't decide whether to laugh or curse. What else would this unfortunate day bring? That addled old crone worshipped her brother. The brother she was trying to escape. Alrek Bjørnsson, self-proclaimed jarl of their clan. Marta considered him an enlightened god. Adellis bowed her head, wishing Fate had cast its lots in her favor for a change.

Many of the villagers on Mull adored her charismatic twin, and Adellis would be the first to admit that Alrek's greatest talent was weaving lies that could charm dogs away from meat. His latest quest was to return the Hebrides to Norway and void the Treaty of Perth. He saw it as a means of obtaining more power. The calculating fool hungered for power and status, often claiming the gods had placed him in the wrong age. Alrek longed for the conquering times of old, the eras regaled in the Viking sagas.

Marta's appearance made her gnaw harder on the leather between her teeth. She had believed capture by the *Gallóglaigh* an effective, albeit distasteful, way of escaping her brother and starting a new life in Scotland. Now she had to deal with Marta, who would report everything she heard and saw. Adellis felt certain of it. Alrek would attempt to retrieve her, and if he succeeded, would curtail her movements even more. Or kill her. With Alrek, anything was possible.

"You have ruptured the old wound," Marta muttered in their native tongue as she bent close. With a meaningful nod, she squeezed Adellis's leg as though offering reassurance that all would be reported, and a rescue would happen. "She be wounded," she announced, for the benefit of the one called Thorburn. Or Thor. Or m'lord or Constable. Adellis had lost count of the mighty Scottish bear's many names.

Her captor lifted his hulking body off the stool, flinching as the weight of his muscular bulk strained the venom-laced puncture she had inflicted to his knee. She knew all about the *Gallóglaigh*. Rapists. Thieves. Destroyers. They had no honor. Sold their battle prowess to the highest bidder, no matter the cause. It made her ashamed that these massive savages had descended from mixing the blood of her Viking ancestors with lowly Highlanders. But this man was a means to her end.

"Mend her," the great beast ordered the healer.

Amazing. This one appeared concerned about her welfare. That didn't fit with what she knew of these warriors. Why would he care about her wound? He could still abuse her. If the gag didn't have her mouth locked in place, she would have smiled. Although, whenever he did attempt his ravaging, that knee should burn fierce enough to soften his cock. That would buy her a bit of time before she had to endure his brutality. She refused to dwell on how she would be used. Anything could be endured for freedom. A means to an end, she reminded herself. Freedom was worth it.

He limped over to stand beside the healer and scowled down at her injury. She felt like prey caught in a snare.

With a curved knife, Marta cut away the leg of her trews, revealing the festering gash high on her hip. She had received the wicked slice from none other than her brother. He had told her if she insisted on warring like the honorable Viking women of old, then she must prove herself a fitting tribute to them on a regular basis.

The vicious cur had taken to poisoning his blade whenever

they parried. Not enough to kill her, but a toxin known to slow healing. It was her punishment for refusing his order to seduce his rivals and murder them at first opportunity. She shared her favors for pleasure and her own benefit. Also for protection. But as her brother's power grew, so did the dangers. She had to escape him and his reach before it was too late.

"That is an old wound," the Scot observed. "She'll be needing whisky for when ye scrape it." Before Marta could answer, he turned and bellowed, "Hendry. Whisky. Plenty of it."

"And how is she to drink for the pain?" the healer asked.

"Convince her to stop her spitting, and ye can remove that gag of hers."

Marta gave a chiding click of her tongue, then tapped on Adellis's leg. "You must not spit. This will not be pleasant without the constable's whisky."

Adellis agreed with a regal bow of her head. She wondered if the Scot knew that, unlike *Gallóglaigh*, when she gave her word, it meant something. Relieved of the wadded knot of leather, she worked her jaws and made a pointless effort of wetting her lips.

Hendry appeared with a swollen leather skin and another cup, eyeing her as though she suffered from the plague. He handed the articles to the crone and backed away. Adellis rubbed her mouth to hide her amusement. That one better hope his slavery to the Scottish bear lasted a lifetime. Soft and cowardly as he was, he would never survive without his master.

"Drink," Marta ordered. "All."

Adellis wondered if Marta always chopped her speech whenever around the Scots. Why would she do so? To make them feel superior? After enjoying a deep breath of the alcohol's heady fumes, she downed the liquid fire in one satisfying gulp.

"Another." She held out the cup, startled when her captor laughed.

"Give her all she wants," he ordered. "Her leg looks festered to the bone."

"When you start the cleaning, give me back the gag," Adellis told Marta, enjoying the hot glow in her gullet, and determined to keep it well fueled.

"There is no shame in crying out, lass," the Scot assured her, grunting as he bent to retrieve the bit of leather and handed it to her.

"I was speaking to the healer."

"Aye. I know." He gave her a disarming smile. Damn him. Viking heritage ran strong in this Highlander, blessing him with everything that attracted her to those sorts of men. Or maybe it was the drink softening her. Nay. It was him. That hair, bright as gold glinting in the sunlight. Eyes like the sea. Stormy blue ever-changing with shifting shadows. Strong cut features. The perfection of his sternness was offset by a dimple in his left cheek when he smiled. A sign the gods had touched him whilst he swam in his mother's womb. No wonder some called him Thor. He could pass for the Viking god himself.

"Who are ye, lass?" he asked as he pulled the stool closer and sat.

"I am not a lass." She drained the cup again before adding, "I am a woman you had best be wary of." She caught Marta's subtle smile out of the corner of her eye.

The Scot had the gall to give a gallant bow of his head. "Forgive me, m'lady. I am Thorburn MacDougall. Might I know yer name to address ye proper?"

"Drink more," Marta ordered as she shoved the refilled cup into her hands and gave the slightest shake of her head. The old healer didn't wish her to say her name. Why? Her brother was only a fearsome legend in his own imaginings and among some of the villagers. How dare this misguided user of herbs try to curb her.

She downed the drink and held it out for another, then rolled to her side so the crone could better work on her hip. With her head propped in one hand, she glared up at Thorburn. "Adellis Bjørnsdóttir."

"Adellis," he repeated.

Marta scraped a blade across the ruptured wound.

Adellis flinched and gritted her teeth to keep from cursing aloud. She grabbed hold of the old woman's wrist and stopped her before she could make another pass. "More drink first."

"There is not enough drink in this world to grant ye the oblivion you seek," the healer hissed.

"Do ye know this woman?" Suspicion echoed in the Scot's tone.

"Nay, Constable." The scowling matron recovered quickly. "I can tell her handling of drink by the way she acts." She waved him back. "I would see your wounds next, my lord. Young Hendry said the knee was the worst. Prepare yourself as I finish with this one. I will not be long."

Adellis tossed the empty cup aside and held out her hand. "Give me the Scot's whisky. The bag of it."

"Thorburn," he corrected as he stripped off his tunic. With a tip of his head, he winked. "Or Thor. That's what some call me. Use it, if ye prefer."

"Blasphemy," Marta muttered under her breath, but Adellis plainly heard it.

Adellis took another long draught of the painkilling spirits, then smiled as the delicious burn flooded her veins. "We are Christian now, old woman. Remember?"

Marta's sour look tightened. She didn't reply, but the iciness in her watery eyes promised that every word, every action, would be reported to Jarl Alrek. Adellis read it as plain as black ink on fresh parchment.

After another hard pull on the leather flask, she corked it and set it aside. "Do it," she ordered, then shoved the leather between her teeth and bit down hard. To keep her mind off the searing pain, she concentrated on the half-naked Scot in front of her.

The dusting of hair on his chest was darker than that on his head. It shadowed the hard cut of his muscles, making him look even more sculpted and shaped for strength and beauty. He had fought much. But the scars didn't mar his perfection, just attested to his power. She found the rugged lines of his hulking mass most pleasing. With that knee wound, he would soon remove the trews. She looked forward to seeing the rest.

A burning wetness splatted onto her hip, making her bite into the leather harder. Fool healer. This was the third time the witch had dressed the wound with that nasty concoction per Alrek's orders. It would also be the last. Adellis would again tend to it herself as soon as she could obtain what she needed.

"Lift your leg," Marta ordered. She wound a stained linen strip around the thigh to keep the green muck in place. With a huffing grunt, the old one pushed herself to her feet and turned to the Scot. "All of it," she said, pointing at his bloodstained trews.

Adellis helped herself to another drink, then held the flask out to him.

He accepted it with a smile, took a long hard pull on it, then handed it back. With a pained grunt, he shoved off the trews, then lowered the finest set of buttocks Adellis had ever seen back down to the stool. Every time the Scot moved, the play of his muscles created a mesmerizing display of taut, flexing manliness. She had enjoyed her share of lovers, but none had displayed the generous wares this man offered. Generous. Yes. A very appropriate description. And that was even while the length of it lay flaccid across his thigh.

With a knowing smirk and the arch of a brow, he shifted to improve her view. His sleeping member awakened, hardening enough to lift its thickness in polite greeting. This one would be a most satisfying lover, indeed. Perhaps that would be a surer way of winning an escape to Scotland rather than traveling as a slave to be given to the man's liege. Seduction rather than submission. And this seduction wouldn't be the act of a cowardly assassin. If all went well, it could make her final disappearance easier once they reached Scotland. A trusted woman, the lover of the *Gallóglaigh* Constable, would wear no shackles.

The man didn't flinch as Marta removed the arrow from his shoulder, just stared straight ahead as though deep in thought.

The missile hadn't gone deep. While his chain mail hadn't stopped it completely, it had slowed it enough to prevent severe damage. When the crone moved to the oozing puncture just above his knee, Adellis pushed herself upward to better see. She didn't trust Marta to treat the injury properly. Not as devoted as the old woman was to Alrek. The healer might have won the warrior's trust by aiding them in the past, but that could be his undoing. Especially now.

"It must be laid open from knee to ankle," the crone advised as she reached for her blade.

"No." Adellis drew as close as her chains would allow. "Do not cut him. Flush the hole with whisky, then pack it with honey and wrap it."

"Are ye a healer, lass—" He cut himself off and bowed his head. "Are ye a healer, Lady Adellis?" he amended.

While she appreciated him elevating her to the status of lady, she ignored it. Instead, she stared at the old woman, daring her to speak to the contrary. "No. But when there was no healer, I tended my own wounds in the way I mentioned, and they healed."

"The poison has spread," Marta argued, her intense glare shouting for Adellis to back down and shut her mouth.

"The venom I used is not lethal." Adellis pointed at his foot. "Has the feeling not already returned?"

He wiggled his toes, then tilted his head. "Aye, it has. Almost normal now." With a tap of his finger atop his knee, he gave Marta a stern look. "Do as she said rather than split it open. Whisky, then the honey."

"I have no honey, and it must be treated now. She is mistaken about the poisons." The determined healer lifted her sharp chin. "You risk your life by placing your trust in a prisoner who would benefit by your death."

The old woman was creative, but she did not lie well. Adellis allowed herself a faint smile. Even the Scot knew the hag lied. She could see it in his eyes.

"Hendry!" the warrior bellowed as he rested an elbow on the table beside him.

"Aye, m'lord?"

The boy appeared carrying a tray laden with steaming platters and bowls smelling so good that Adellis's stomach growled. The Scot had promised to feed her if she behaved. Surely, saving his leg counted for that.

"We need honey," she told Hendry. "And boiled linens and clean bandages."

The Highland bear smiled. "Aye, Hendry. Do as the lady says." Before the knave had the chance to fetch the items, he added, "And give Marta a groat for her troubles as ye show her out."

"Tomorrow, I return and check your prisoner." The furious woman fixed Adellis with a tight-lipped scowl that warned Alrek would not be pleased.

"If the constable permits," Adellis said. "I will make use of whatever honey he has no need for. Your return will not be necessary."

"There will be plenty of honey," Thorburn promised with a regal dip of his chin. His gaze slid back to Marta. "Yer services are no longer needed here, ye ken?"

With a huffing growl, the crone knotted the black shawl around her poultices and tools and scuttled out of the tent.

"With her as your healer, I am surprised any of you are still alive," Adellis observed, wondering how long it would take the old woman to make it to Alrek and tell him all she knew.

"Ye sound certain, and yet she swore she had never met ye."

His hawklike focus burned into her. The man would recognize a poorly crafted lie and pounce. She had to be careful.

"I have seen her among us." She lifted her chin and met his scrutiny head on. "But more, I will not say." There. That placed the lies on the witch, not her.

"And why would ye protect me from her?" He shifted on the stool.

"Allowing an old woman to cripple one's enemy is a coward's way out. Not mine."

He smiled, but she could tell by the look in his eyes, he wasn't fully convinced. No matter. She would win him and use him soon enough.

Hendry returned with a cloth-covered crock in one hand and a steaming pot in the other. "Honey and boiled linens, m'lord." He set both on the table, pulled a bundle of rolled strips out of the apron tied around his waist, and placed them on the table.

"I would wash that muck from his shoulder and use the whisky and honey there as well."

Adellis shifted positions to unwind the filthy wrap the hag had placed on her leg. Weary and disgusted with the piss-soaked trews, she kicked the chains between her feet out of the way, stood, and ripped away what remained of the soiled garment. Urinating on her captor had not been one of her better battle tactics. She shook her tunic back down to her knees, then wadded up the ruined trews and tossed them to the open ground beside the tent wall. It was a small area left uncovered by furs or tapestries. She assumed that was where they intended her to relieve herself since a pot hadn't been provided.

When she turned back to see if they might spare some of the boiled linens and a bandage, neither male had moved. Hendry stood with his mouth ajar. The Scottish bear stared at her as though she were his next meal. Her gaze slid to his lap, and she suppressed a smile. His impressive shaft had risen completely, standing rigid and tall, ready for a more active part in the conversation. She pretended not to notice, priding herself on the mastery of controlling her expressions and keeping her thoughts to herself. It had saved her life many a time.

Instead, she set her focus on the steaming pot, then shifted her gaze to Hendry. "You should clean away the witch's mud before it dries. It will pain him less that way."

Hendry blinked as though waking from a dream. "Aye, m'lady."

She wished her chains could reach the table. That food was getting cold. Cheese. Bread. The nicely browned leg of that bird. Some of the boiled meat. Smother it all in that brown gravy. She licked her lips.

Without a word, her captor scooped up a plate and filled it with what looked like the choicest bits as Hendry struggled to wash his shoulder.

Adellis swallowed hard, trying not to drown in her own saliva. She lowered herself to a cross-legged position on the furs, hoping that once the Scot ate his fill, he might offer her the scraps. After all, she had not only saved his leg but also given him a full viewing of hers. The seduction would take time to work its magic and place her at the table beside him, but eventually, she would get there. For now, scraps would keep her alive.

"Here, lass," he said, holding out the plate. The dimple in his cheek deepened with his lopsided smile. "Sorry. Yer plate, m'lady."

"Perhaps lass is not so offensive," she said, accepting the surprising offer with graceful restraint. She didn't wish to appear as starving and grateful as a mongrel begging for its master's favor.

"Nay, it is not meant to offend." He sucked in a hissing breath as Hendry poured some of the whisky on his shoulder injury.

"Blow on it," she instructed between bites.

"What?" With the cup of whisky held over the puncture wound on the side of his liege's leg, Hendry stared at her.

She shrugged. "Blowing on it has always eased the burn when I use it on myself."

After another doubtful wrinkling of his nose, the lad sloshed more whisky on the puncture, then blew on it until he looked about to drop.

"That is plenty," she said, sopping up the thick, rich gravy with a crusty chunk of bread. She wolfed down the last of the boiled meat, contemplated licking the plate, then decided against it. They might consider Norwegians as uncivilized as animals, but that didn't mean she had to act the part. After topping off her meal by draining the tankard of ale her intriguing keeper had placed within reach, she fixed a knowing look at him. "Well? Did it help?"

His amazement clear, the Scot nodded. "Aye, it did." He tipped his head at her now empty plate, the lopsided grin wider this time. "More?"

"Nay." She handed him the plate and cup. "But I thank you." With teasing slowness, she inched her tunic higher, then curled to expose her wounded hip. "But if a boiled cloth could be spared, I would be grateful."

With his stare locked on the length of her leg, he wet his mouth like a man starving for a last meal.

For some unknown reason, her legs had always been admired by her lovers. She pointed her toes and stretched, making a pretense of examining her wound from a different angle. She had never understood the fascination with her legs. Between them was a man's ultimate goal.

"Hendry," he rasped without pulling his gaze away. "Anything the lady needs, aye?"

With an obedient bob of his head, the lad set the crock of honey on the table and hefted the bail of the iron pot containing the steaming linens. He set it beside her and added one of the rolls of clean bandages beside it.

She cleaned the healer's filth from the wound, gritting her teeth against the pain. The old woman's muddy herbs always made the gash worse, which was probably why Alrek insisted the crone tend her. He never allowed the hag near any of his injuries. She wrung out a clean cloth and held it up. "Would you soak this in whisky?" she asked Hendry.

The lad dipped his chin as he finished winding a cloth around the Scot's knee. "A moment, and I will."

"Here, lass." Her captor poured some whisky into a bowl and held it out.

Again, his kind helpfulness surprised her as well as set her on edge. What was wrong with this Highland commander? Was this a game for him? Some sort of tactic to throw her off guard; then he would turn cruel and wicked later? Or did he realize she played a game of seduction, and this was his counterattack? Whatever it was, she would go carefully and plan well. Her freedom depended on it.

The burn of the liquid in the already raw gash made her clench her teeth. She fanned away the pain as best she could since she couldn't twist enough to hit it with a good strong breath.

The mighty Scot went down on his good knee and blew on the wound, creating a burn that had nothing to do with whisky.

"I thank you." She managed a smile, struggling to maintain her composure. This one wielded gentleness as dangerously as any weapon.

"Honey." He held out his hand without looking away from her.

Hendry placed the vessel in his hand. "Yer food grows cold, m'lord. I can dress her wound if ye wish."

"Nay." The man's grin was gone, replaced by a much more calculating slant. "I will tend her.

With an amazingly light touch, he spread the golden stickiness across the gash, then set the pot aside and bandaged it. She lifted her leg without his even asking, noting that his cock remained rigid, as if supervising his progress. The way the muscles in his jaw kept flexing, she would lay odds he gritted his teeth, too. Good. He was struggling.

"There now," he said as he shoved himself up and returned to his seat. Without another word, he faced the table and started shoving food in his mouth.

What a strange man.

She scooted up to a sitting position, leaned back against the trunk, and watched him. His man Hendry was joined by the gangly lad who had attended him in the woods. Only two servants. Interesting. Her brother didn't attempt to lift a finger without at least a dozen trying to do it for him.

"I went back and gathered up the bits of her armor," Tasgall said. With her chest plate in one hand and the chain mail and leather padding in the other, he shook his head. "I couldna find her helm."

At that announcement, the Scot stopped eating and gave the knave his full attention. "Ye searched the clearing fully?"

"Aye, m'lord." The boy dumped the articles in a corner already filled with weaponry, shields, and tools. "The dead were already gone, too."

"Yer people worked quickly," the warrior observed, a pensiveness to his tone. "Almost as if they watched while ye were taken and the others sent to the next life."

She fully agreed but wasn't about to let him know it. Instead, she remained silent.

His nostrils flared as though testing the air for the stench of a lie. He turned back to his food. "Well done, Tasgall. Go to yer supper now, then find yer rest. More hot water, Hendry, then ye may go as well."

Both knaves bobbed their heads, then left.

So, it begins, she thought. She braced herself, wondering if this was where the true man came to light.

Silence filled the tent. Well, not exactly silence. The sounds of the men outside filtered in: muffled conversations and muted movements. Candles sputtered as wind gusted against the heavy cloth of the temporary dwelling. The Scot's knife scraped against his metal plate. Clanked, then scraped. Repeatedly. And he chewed as loud as a horse chomping green apples. A sensitivity to sound had always been her curse. She had the hearing of a bat. While it served her well both on the battlefield and everyday survival, the trait tormented her, too. Nightfall would come soon, bringing with it a welcomed peacefulness—perhaps.

Thorburn. She toyed with the name, rolling it around in her mind as the man who bore it rose from the table and stretched. His fingertips brushed the ceiling of the tent. No. *Thorburn* did not fit this man. Thor. Or Bear. Much more fitting. He would be so to her from now on.

"How many, Adellis?" he asked as he washed, then donned the clean tunic that the one called Hendry had draped across the massive sleeping platform along the far wall of the tent.

"If I tell you anything, when they recover me, I will be flayed and left for the terns." That part wasn't a lie nor part of the seduction. If Alrek suspected her of betrayal, it wouldn't matter that she was his only kin.

"They willna recover ye." He lowered himself to sit on the edge of the platform, studying her as though she were an animal he had never encountered before. "The healer. One of yer number?"

"She wishes to be." She would tell him that much. Doing so would ban Marta from the camp and prevent further interference from her. Rising to her feet, she stretched just as he had, knowing the action would hike her shift high enough to tease. The movement wasn't wasted. His gaze locked on her hemline and stayed there until she lowered her arms.

The chains of her shackles clinking, she undid her braids, then raked her fingers through her hair, letting it fall down her back in a wild cascade of wavy ringlets. Men loved her long hair as much as they loved her legs. Who knew why? She turned her back to him and continued untangling her tresses.

Some in her clan considered her whorish, but she preferred to think of herself as a woman who knew what she wanted and how to get it. Her carefully selected lovers had not only foiled her brother's plan at bartering her virginity for an advantageous marriage, but the men she had chosen had also somewhat protected her from his wrath. At least for a little while. Unfortunately, as his power grew, her lovers became less protective, forcing her to find other options. Escape from her twin was her only hope for a life that wouldn't make her slit her own throat.

She allowed herself a faint smile as the heat of the man told her he stood close behind her. Impressive. She hadn't heard a sound. Bracing herself, she waited. Would the bear attack, or would gentleness continue to rule?

He combed his fingers through her hair. "As silky as it looks," he breathed, then gently but firmly turned her to face him. His brows were the light golden brown of oat sheafs. They knotted over his narrowed eyes as he stared down at her. "Ye are a beauty, m'lady."

"You are a bear, m'lord." She never flattered lovers. She challenged them. The comment won her a smile.

"A weary bear," he said as he brushed the curve of her cheek with the backs of his fingers. His hand dropped away, and he stepped back and made a formal bow. "I bid ye good evening and pleasant rest, m'lady."

Without waiting for a response, he retired to his bed and gave her his back.

Amazed and slightly insulted, she stared at him, watching the ever-slowing rise and fall of his side as his breathing settled into the rhythm of a man deep within his dreams. How dare he spurn her! She had seen his rigid cock. He clearly wanted her. What the devil was his game?

Fuming, she reclined on the furs and stared up at the shadows dancing across the tent. She had thought to challenge him, but instead, he had challenged her. Fine. Never let it be said that Adellis Bjørnsdóttir ever backed down from a challenge.

CHAPTER THREE

G OD HELP HIM to hold fast.

Her presence teased him like a delicious meal ready to be devoured while her irritated fuming charged the air until it crackled. Her repeated low mutterings, indiscernible as a witch's chant, hissed through the shadows. The chains of her shackles softly clinked the entire time.

He prided himself on his powerful restraint and control, but she threatened both. A yearning stronger than the need to breathe possessed him, and the minx damn well knew it.

When he had ordered Tasgall to stake the fiery temptress in his tent, he had never expected the show she would provide. He sensed she wouldn't cower, but never had he thought she would toy and tease. 'Twas more than a little obvious; the lady believed that all *Gallóglaigh* warriors thought with nothing other than their cocks. And many did. But not him. Even though this night he wished he could. But nay, he could not trust her. She would use any of his weaknesses to escape.

Another of her deep huffing sighs made him swallow hard. She continued with whatever she was doing longer than he ever expected. Probably angry because he foiled whatever plot she stewed. He struggled to keep his breathing slow and steady to convince her he slept as deeply as a babe in its mother's arms. Thank God above that Tasgall had staked her with a chain too short to reach his bed. If she stayed out of his reach, he might get through this night without succumbing to the wants of his aching manparts.

"*Jævla* templar," she muttered, then it sounded like she spit. Probably at him, no doubt.

He had to hold his breath to keep from laughing. If that word meant what he thought it meant, she had just called him a *feckin' templar*. Not bloody likely. He was far from being celibate as a monk. And if all went as he planned, she would discover that for herself. But not just yet. Not before a bit of trust had grown between them. As of right now, he considered her a cunning adversary, willing to make use of any weapon at her disposal—and her current weaponry was more powerful than any blade.

Her irons clinked louder, accompanied by what he thought sounded like a muted grunt. A moment of silence, then whatever she was up to repeated itself, followed by more Norwegian mutterings. While he didn't understand what she said, he would bet his best dagger her words weren't the language of a proper lady. The need to know what she was doing nagged at him. If he rolled to his stomach as though shifting in his sleep, he could turn his head without her thinking him awake. Aye, that was a plan.

At the next rattling of her shackles, he moved, adding a low mumbling groan to lend a more realness to the act.

Silence fell faster than an executioner's axe.

He cracked his eyelids the barest slit.

The lovely Adellis was on her feet. Somewhat. The woman had threaded the chain of her wrist shackles around or through the chains connecting her ankles to the post. He couldn't tell for certain because of the shadows. The sputtering candles from earlier had nearly burned out. Only a few remained lit. Frozen in a defensive crouch, she watched him. Waiting. It looked as though her current plan depended on leveraging the stakes out of the ground.

He admired her determination but wondered at the plot. Did she mean to escape under the tent wall or through the door? Let him live or kill him in his sleep? Of course, a proper warrior would kill him. He supposed if she succeeded in slipping out of the camp, the nearby village would get her back to her clan. The craftsmanship of her armor showed her people knew enough about metalworking to rid her of the shackles. That is—if she made it that far. The encampment of his twoscore and ten warriors would be quite the snare to escape.

Apparently, after satisfying herself that he still slept, she started rocking back and forth while pulling on the chains. Good tactic. Since Tasgall had hammered the pair of stakes at opposing angles, she had her work cut out for her. It all depended on the willingness of the ground to release the twisted bits of iron that were the length of a man's forearm.

With a disgruntled huff, she plopped down on her shapely arse, untangled her wrists from her feet, and propped her arms atop her bent knees. Poor lass had worked herself out of breath. Either that or decided the effort futile. He couldn't stand it any longer. Pushing up from the bed, he made his way to the table and divided what was left in the pitcher of ale between two tankards.

"Here." He offered her one, unable to keep from grinning at the daggers in her eyes. Lord help him, what a delightful mix of fire and ice she was. "Were ye able to loosen them at all?"

"Brenne i helvete!"

"If ye are going to curse at me, do ye not feel it would be more effective if I understood ye?"

"Burn in. hell," she repeated, drained the tankard, then threw it at his head.

He easily dodged the cup before finishing off his own. "I probably will burn for all I have done."

"I will be there with you." She blew out a heavy sigh and propped her chin back on her forearms.

The wily temptress from earlier had disappeared, leaving in her place a quiet, pensive woman. Perhaps her thinking him celibate as a monk might enable a truthful conversation between them. He lowered himself to one knee but remained ready to retreat should it prove necessary. He trusted neither her nor himself.

"Who are ye, Adellis Bjørnsdóttir? Why do ye waste yerself in such a useless fight?" For that was what this was. These small incursions to void a treaty that had already lasted seven years? Madness itself. Besides, little changed for the tiny Isle of Mull, no matter what kingdom held it.

"I battle for the same reason you do," she answered while staring off into the darkness. "My life and my sword belong to my liege."

"And who is yer liege?"

Whether it was from the failing light or her sagging spirits, another dimension to her loveliness made itself known. She suddenly looked years older. No less comely, but somehow less fierce than before. A haggardness shrouded her. Something akin to a flinch escaped her before she wrestled her control back into place. "My liege is my brother, Alrek Bjørnsson."

Thorburn knew the name. That fool still claimed allegiance to Haakon even though Magnus, King Haakon's son, now ruled Norway. But where Haakon had been an aggressive and warring monarch, Magnus politicked and bartered. He had traded away the Hebrides, not only saving resources but gaining a fine bit of silver in the process. "Magnus denounces yer brother's actions. The agreement between Scotland and Norway has thrived for years now. What can he possibly hope to gain?"

"What all men crave." She rubbed the corners of her eyes, then pulled her focus from the darkness and settled it on him. "Power." Her tone made the word more lethal.

"He seeks power by controlling wee Mull?" He couldn't stop a disbelieving grunt. "Is yer brother that great a fool?"

"My brother believes himself to be the Viking descendent meant to revive their glory." The woman sounded ready to spit again. It was clear she bore no admiration or love for her brother.

"Why do ye serve him?" The question begged to be asked.

Her features hardened, and the ice returned to her eyes. "My brother's grasp is not an easy one to slip. Especially since I am female." A side-eyed look toward the tent's exit tightened her mouth, pulling it into a frown. "Even now, I promise you, he plans to recover me. Not because I am his sister, but his chattel. And the healer you called forth will ensure my return is less than pleasant."

"Why?"

"Because she worships Alrek as a god." She reclined across the furs and curled over onto her side. With her head pillowed on her arm, she stared straight ahead at nothing at all. "She feeds the sickness of his mind." With a twitch of a shoulder, she added, "I would lay odds she reported I prevented her from crippling the skilled warrior who cost him so many of his best archers." Another deep breath left her in a dismal sigh. "Although, their deaths lay at my door as well. I set our defenses poorly." After rubbing her eyes again, she shooed him away with a flip of her hand. "Go. Sleep. The rattle of my chains will trouble you no more, great bear."

Great bear? From her, he rather liked that. "If you had escaped, where would you have gone?" It didn't sound as though she planned on returning to her clan or the village.

She rolled to her other side, giving him her back. "I did not seek escape," she replied through a hitching yawn. "I sought to join you in your bed."

"Why?"

"Are you *sakte* as well as *sølibat?*"

"Am I what?" The one word resembled celibate, but the other?

She twisted to face him and pinned him with a damning glare. "Forgive me. Weariness returns me to my native tongue. I asked you if you were *slow* as well as *celibate*." Without waiting for his reaction, she flopped away again and settled deeper into the furs.

"I am neither slow nor celibate," he defended to her back. "But I still dinna allow the wants of my cock to risk me or my men."

Silence fell between them. Her slow breathing made him think she had found their conversation so dull that she had fallen asleep in the middle of it. Just when he thought to return to his bed, she rolled to her back and looked at him.

"I am no longer a threat to you or your men." Her confession came out as an irritated hiss, causing him to seat himself beside her pallet. Her tensed smile was as bitter as her tone. "I meant to seduce you, oh mighty Thorburn. Use you. Gain your trust so you might protect me with your warriors and take me back to the mainland when you left Mull. *Then* I planned to escape and disappear deep into Scotland. Perhaps, even farther."

"Why did ye not tell me that back in the woods?" She had not held back in her fight, and he knew, if he had faltered, she would have killed him.

"Because those who fought against you would have just as easily turned their arrows on me." Her tone held no fear or rancor. She talked of her own forces killing her as if it was something as ordinary as the weather.

Behind all her hardness, all her ferocity, and every bit of her seductive posturing hid a forlorn soul seeking sanctuary. He reached out and touched the cool silk of her cheek.

She stared up at him. Watchful. Waiting. Silent.

Such full lips, he thought as he ran the tip of his thumb across them. When she didn't move, he withdrew and stared down at her. He had never met such a woman.

"You would have enjoyed my interruption of your celibacy," she informed him with a dip of her chin.

"Of that, I have no doubt." He could no longer resist all that was her. Not just her body. But her indomitable and yet somehow fragile spirit as well. Gingerly straightening his sore knee, he stretched out beside her.

She shifted to her side. Facing him, the waning candlelight danced in her eyes. Her sweat, her intoxicating musk, even the hint of ale on her breath fanned the fires in his blood. The glimmer of a smile danced across the mouth that would soon be his.

"I have never had a Scottish bear before," she observed.

"Dare I risk ye, my lovely Adellis?" He treated himself to the inviting curve of her graceful throat. Salty. Smooth as velvet. The quickening of her lifeblood tapped against his lips as he grazed them across her flesh—such an addictive beginning.

"Dare you not?" she breathed into his ear, her tone as teasing as her touch. She tickled her fingers across the part of him where her gaze had lingered once he removed his trews. The coolness of her chains slid along his thighs as she became more brazen. Stroking. Squeezing. "And how shall we do this, my Viking god?"

He drew back from enjoying the delicious breast he had glimpsed earlier. "How?"

She ceased her exquisite massaging and held up her hands. "Shackled. Chained. Staked." With a wicked dip of her lashes, she lightly pressed a leg against his bandaged knee. "And you a hobbled steed."

Suspicion dampened his lust just enough to give him pause. He edged back the slightest bit. "Answer me this. Would ye release a prisoner ye had only just captured?" He smoothed his hand across her hip and squeezed the buttock he had known would be wondrous and firm. "Even if ye did feel as though a bit of trust might be growing between the two of ye?"

"Fair enough." After a glance at her ankle chained closest to the stake, she smiled and slid her gaze back to his. "Get beneath me and scoot downward with your legs on either side of the rods. Straddle them if you will."

"Why?"

"Because I mean to ride you and need enough slack for a proper mounting." She leaned forward and flicked the tip of her tongue along his collarbone as she increased the pace of her squeezing pulls. "And I warn you, my gait is a gallop. Not a slow, gentle trot," she said softly, the tickling of her breath searing his skin.

Saints preserve him; he could feel his heartbeat pounding in his bollocks.

She pushed herself to her feet and lifted the hem of her léine, revealing the long, lean form of a warrior enhanced by the tempting breasts and delectable arse of a master seductress. The candlelight painted her golden. Visions of her riding him made it harder to breathe.

"Come to me, my bear," she coaxed with a fluttering of her fingers. "Let us enjoy this bit of heaven granted to us lowly mortals."

He had known by the way she had battled him that her passions would be just as rare and breathtaking. This was not a woman who grudgingly pleasured a man because he wished it. This sparring goddess demanded pleasuring for herself, as well. But survival instincts held him in check. Beneath her, she could use those chains for a darker purpose. Fear of harm didn't allay him. Nay, something else held him back—the potential damage to their fragile understanding. Their trust was new. It hadn't fully blossomed yet but was very close. He wouldn't risk shattering it.

Rising from the floor, he took a step back.

An immediate leeriness appeared in her stance. Chin lifting to a defiant tilt, she yanked down her shirt and covered herself. "You mean to refuse me. Again."

"Nay, lass." He took the stool from beside the table, placed it alongside the stakes, and sat. "I willna refuse ye again, but neither will I toss all caution to the winds." He opened his knees wider and pulled her in between them. "More control this way, aye?"

"More control?" she repeated, resting her hands on his shoulders. Her chains slid across his chest, snagging in the hairs and pinching. "You thought I planned to use my bonds against you?"

"It had occurred to me." With his hands molding her buttocks and the tautness of her warm stomach brushing his chin and nose, he struggled to explain further. Before he could find the words, she turned within his embrace and faced outward.

"For trust," she explained, lifting her tunic again to display her delightful backside. Without a moment's hesitation, she lowered herself into his lap, engulfing him with a hard downward shove that made him groan. "There, my hesitant bear," she said, flexing as she lay back against his chest. "My chains are of no danger to you this way."

"Trust me, m'lady," he said while palming a breast and reaching around to slide his fingers along the silkiness of her inner thigh. "I still find ye verra dangerous."

"Good," she purred, moving her hips in slow, exquisite circles. She guided his touch to the slippery heat of their joining, covering his hand with her own. Her fingers told him what she wanted—nay, not wanted, but demanded. With their united, artful massaging, her hips pumped harder, rewarding him for the effort. The lady had said she wished a hard gallop, then a hard gallop she would have. The stool creaked beneath them, risking collapse. He didn't care. More room on the floor.

That realization fueled an insatiable need for such freedom, forcing him to stand and bend her to her hands and knees in front of him. He vaguely noticed the pain in his leg, but it was fleeting. More enjoyable sensations demanded his attention. He fully embraced them, pounding with a fury. She served him well, adding to the dance by arching back against him and meeting him thrust for thrust. It was no longer a dance but a battle between them. Passion against passion. Need vying with need. By the time they collapsed in the furs, neither could speak. Just held each other while gasping and heaving for air.

"Well done, my fine bear." She pecked a kiss to his inner arm, then pillowed her head upon it as he curled around her.

"And ye as well, m'lady." With his fingers tucked between her breasts, he grazed a kiss across her shoulder, then buried his face in the silkiness of her hair. Every movement took extra effort. It was as though the air itself weighed him down, and he was too weak to fight it.

She nestled back tighter against his chest, then went still. Her breathing slowed and, for the first time since he had set eyes on the enticing wee fury, she relaxed, melting into him with the softness of a bairn's rag doll.

He should sleep, too, but his conscience wouldn't allow it. While he hadn't forced himself upon the lass, he had most definitely used her. What others thought didn't worry him. Much. The respect of his men mattered. Respect unified his warriors and made them fight as a single powerful force. But if they decided him a hypocrite for not only taking a prisoner but also helping himself to all she offered? What then? What would happen to his order that no women or children ever be harmed or abused?

And what of her? The more he thought over what little she had finally shared, the more he decided this fierce beauty needed saving, whether she realized it or not. Life had made her depend on only herself. Necessity had forced her to seek them out for aid in the fight for her freedom. He wondered if she realized how fortunate she was to have crossed paths with them rather than *Gallóglaighs* from a different clan. The mercenaries were known for their brutality for a reason. Even within the MacDougall clan, some questioned his ability to lead because of his mindset regarding women, children, or any of the weak, for that matter. But he set them straight with such a fury, no one ever questioned him again.

He closed his eyes and nuzzled deeper into her hair.

"Be still," she mumbled, pulling his arm tighter around her. "Sleep."

He smiled at the scolding. A dangerous warmth, something akin to contentment, flickered into existence and spread through him like the burn of good whisky. Aye, she was a dangerous one indeed, needing no weapon other than her spirit. The weight of weariness set in and pushed him closer to oblivion.

Tomorrow, he would come up with a plan. For now, he would do as he was told.

A WHIMPERING SHOUT and a body thrashing against him jerked him to full wakefulness.

"*Nei! Nei!*" She twisted away, both hands lifted as though fending off blows. Even by the dim light of a lone candle, the misery twisting her features was unmistakable. Eyes squeezed shut, she rolled and flailed, battling the attacker only she could see. Vicious demons haunted her dreams.

He dodged the irons as she fought, trying to wake her gently. "Adellis!" Catching hold of her chains, he pulled them taut and spoke louder. "Wake yerself, lass. Adellis!"

Chest heaving, skin glistening with sweat, she opened her eyes and became still. "I am sorry I woke you," she rasped, then jerked the chains out of his hands and scooted as far from him as her restraints allowed.

Survivor of a few night horrors of his own, Thorburn lightly rested a hand on her shoulder. She stiffened, making him wish he hadn't touched her. "Are ye all right, lass? Truly?"

"I am fine." She twitched away from his hand and resettled her head on her folded arm. "Just silliness. Like a child dreaming of monsters."

"It is nay silliness when the evil is so real ye can taste it."

She didn't answer, just blew out a shuddering sigh.

"There is no shame in it, ye ken?"

"I am not ashamed of anything," she snapped, then cast an apologetic glance back over her shoulder. "I am not ashamed," she amended in a softer tone while holding his gaze. "But I regret much." Her back still to him, she settled down again, once more nestling her head in the crook of her arm.

"We all regret much." Unable to help himself, he smoothed a wandering tress back in place without even grazing her tunic. "Let me hold ye," he whispered. "I will do my best to keep yer evils at bay."

She turned and fixed him with a hard glare. "Go to sleep. I am fine."

The leeriness in her tone added to the weight of his guilt, the burden he shouldered for rutting her like a beast. It didn't matter that she had seemed willing enough. Perhaps she had only acted so because she feared a brutal ravaging. How could seduction and charm be believed when the woman was chained? A prisoner with no recourse. He pushed himself upward, knowing he would know no peace until he made this right.

Before he could stand, she caught hold of his arm and stopped him. "Why do you rise?"

"Ye will see." Words meant nothing. He would show her. If he had read her truths wrongly, once again, they would do battle, and she would be chained again, but this time in a tent by herself. With a fresh candlestick, he went to Tasgall's corner and sorted through the scattered tools and bits of metal until he found the small curl of iron used to open shackles. He knelt at her feet and removed the irons, then motioned for her hands.

She sat upright but kept her chained hands tucked to her chest. "Why do you do this?"

"Because I am a soft-hearted fool with regrets," he confessed. He held out his hand. "Yer wrists, m'lady."

"You are *Gallóglaigh*, yes?"

"Aye." When she still didn't proffer her remaining bonds, he shifted closer and unlocked the latches. The shackles dropped into her lap.

"Why are you not like the others?" she asked with a quizzical tip of her head toward him.

"I am like the others. I battle the same as they." He knew what she meant. Few understood his edict, which was considered strange and rare among those who called themselves mercenaries. But few had lost their mother and younger sister to such atrocious acts that he and his brothers never spoke of it—not since they had avenged and repaid the horrendous deed. Sometimes, the best way to move forward was to block out the past. He would not speak of it now.

With a satisfied huff, he scooped up the shackles and lobbed them into Tasgall's corner. The key, he left on the table, then returned to his bed rather than his place at her side. Residual guilt walked with him, but with her freedom done, the burden had lightened considerably.

"You are nothing like the others," she said as she rose, still rubbing her wrists.

"If you mean to leave," he advised as he rolled onto his side and faced the wall. "Slip out on the south side of the tent next to the wood. Tasgall and Hendry sleep like the dead on that border. Chances are ye will go unnoticed since the moon isna full."

The ropes of his makeshift sleeping platform creaked as she settled down next to him, hugged herself tightly against his back, and draped an arm around him. "I will not leave."

He covered her arm with his, not entirely sure how he felt about that. He might be better off if she did. "You are certain?"

"I am certain."

Chapter Four

THE WARMTH OF his back against her cheek both soothed and troubled her as she lay awake, staring into the darkness. The springy curls of his chest hair tickled her palm as she slid her hand higher and fitted her legs into the bend behind his knees. For the first time in her life, she was free to do whatever she willed. All because of him. Before she could catch it, a cold shudder of fearful anticipation shook her. She never thought it would, but gaining what she had hoped for so long terrified her.

Breath held, she prayed she hadn't awakened him. After pressing a gentle kiss between his shoulder blades, she pressed her forehead atop it to make sure it reached his soul. "Forgive me," she mouthed, willing him to feel her remorse for using him.

"I canna hear ye, lass," he said quietly, then shifted with a deep inhale and rubbed his calloused hand up and down her arm.

She toyed with a lie, then cast it aside. No. To this man, this honorable Scottish bear, she would never lie. "I asked for you to forgive me."

"Forgive ye?"

"Yes."

"For what?" He rolled to his back while, at the same time, scooping an arm around her. With an endearing huff, he settled her into the dip of his shoulder.

Now she had to explain. She immediately regretted not thinking through all that being honest entailed. "I intended to use you to get what I wanted. In so doing, I have complicated your life."

"My life was already complicated." He paused, then chuckled. "And I would be lying if I said that I didna enjoy the way ye used me. Verra much so."

He hadn't understood all she meant, but that was all right. There was no way to explain. "I enjoyed it, too," she admitted instead.

"Are ye afraid to sleep?" he asked quietly as he rumpled her tunic up out of the way and cupped her bare bottom.

"I have much on my mind." She found a knotted ridge of skin on his chest, a jagged scar just below his heart. "Dagger or spear?"

He slid his fingers up under hers, feeling the spot as though trying to jog his memory. "Ah, that be the one I got in Ireland. He caught me with a spade."

"A landowner?"

"Aye, a father who thought I was the one who ruined his daughter." He shrugged, lifting her head as he did so. "He didna realize I had brought him the man who had."

"Did you force him to marry her?"

"She didna want him." He chuckled and scrubbed his free hand down his face. "Said she hadna even realized he stuck it in her 'til her belly started swelling with his child. Said all he did was flop around on top of her and groan a lot." He laughed harder, shaking them both. "The wee gal said she had already found a man with a much nicer willy. One who owned several sheep and more than one cow. She just needed her Da to come around and agree to the wedding."

Unable to stop it, she snorted out a laugh. "Were you able to convince the man even though he almost killed you?"

"Aye." He rubbed the scar as though the memory made it itch. "It wasna all that deep a wound, and his daughter shamed him in front of half the village. His wife bandaged me up and fed me a fine meal once it was all said and done."

"What happened to your warrior who—" She cleared her throat and tried not to laugh again. "The one who bounced around a lot?"

Thorburn sobered and shifted beneath her with a heavy sigh. "Dead. Fell whilst battling the Normans in Ireland."

"At least he died with honor."

"Aye." He propped a hand behind his head and stared upward. "He did at that."

She tucked in tighter and hugged him with both her arm and the leg she had thrown across him.

"Are ye certain ye're no' afraid to sleep again?"

"Perhaps." She hated admitting any form of weakness, but weariness and the promise she made to herself kept her from lying. "It will be dawn soon, anyway."

He eased over onto his side and faced her. With a featherlight touch, he smoothed her hair away from her face. "Ye dinna have to fear sleeping. I swear to hold ye and stand guard, aye?"

She couldn't help but smile. "Even a mighty warrior such as yourself cannot protect me from my dreams."

"Aye, I can," he argued with all seriousness, adding a tender kiss to his vow. "I shall be yer champion, m'lady. Yer protector. Whether ye be asleep or awake."

She covered his mouth with hers before he could say anything else that would make the dangerous aching in her chest any fiercer. His urgent touch, the taste of him—she concentrated on nothing beyond the sensation every caress invoked. The physical kept her anchored to right now, this moment, where nothing existed but him, the darkness, and the pleasure to be enjoyed.

"You do not mind, do you?" she murmured while arching against him.

He rolled her to her back and settled in place with a hard, possessive thrust that promised to leave the joints of her hips pleasantly sore by morning. "Can ye not tell, m'lady?" he asked, working his hips faster.

The man fit her as though they were interlocking halves that created the perfect whole. She hooked her heels around his legs and pulled. "I believe I can," she teased, raking her nails down his back and digging them into the muscles of his behind.

He bucked harder, just as she wished.

"Good," he rumbled, slowing to catch the lobe of her ear between his teeth. His suckling of it made her swallow hard and wiggle beneath him. He reached down with both hands, clamped hold of her buttocks, and squeezed, yanking her to meet him thrust for thrust. "Good for the goose, good for the gander, aye?"

A shudder kept her from answering. She was so close to delicious oblivion. Had the man just said something about a goose? "You speak of geese?"

"I speak of anything to keep this going for as long as possible," he growled, hammering harder and faster.

"Yes," she agreed. She would agree to anything right now as long as it pushed her into the same wonderful bliss he had given her earlier. "More, my bear. More."

"Aye, m'lady. More, indeed."

THORBURN. THE FIRST word, the first image that filled her mind as soon as Adellis opened her eyes.

She wrinkled her nose as she stared up at the heavy cloth ceiling softly billowing above her. Nay. No matter how hard she tried, that name did not suit the man who had granted her such an unforgettable evening. Thor or her Scottish bear. Those names fit her delightful warrior, her dear, soft-hearted beast. She indulged in a long, luxurious stretch, enjoying the comfort of his bed for a moment longer before pushing herself upright and looking around.

A slow perusal revealed she was alone. Guilt about such slackness on her part pricked at her conscience. How could she have slept so soundly? And without a single dream. The realization made her smile. He had promised to protect her from her demons, and the man had been true to his word.

Even so, whenever Thorburn rose from her side, she should have realized it. But here she sat, staring at what looked like the slant of the midday sun flooding through the open flap of the tent.

Alone. With a pile of clean clothing on the foot of the platform and food and drink within easy reach. She had slept through it all. Both her bear's rustlings and Hendry's service. A disgruntled hiss escaped her. Such laziness was not acceptable at all. Her hands curled into nervous fists. She had never let down her guard like that before. Caution tossed aside not only risked her life but always resulted in chaos. The enjoyment of the fine warrior was fine. Making herself vulnerable to him was not.

When she reached for the tankard, the marks on her wrists reminded her of how he had removed the shackles. She turned and stared at the pile of unlocked irons in the corner. Such a strange man she had found to be her savior. He had even told her the most effective way to escape. The man stirred a troubling confusion within her—no, not confusion, but a strange new weakness she preferred not to examine too closely.

A drink would clear her head. The cool refreshment sloshed against her lips, revealing them chafed and tender this morning. Perhaps from so much use last night? They hadn't kissed all that much, but when they had, it had been with a fierce hunger—not the tender nibbling of hesitant lovers. The memory of it made her ache for him all over again.

The uncomfortable wanting made her resettle herself on the furs. What was wrong with her? She'd enjoyed wonderful lovers before and easily forgotten them when they no longer served her purpose. But none had ever been like her Scottish bear. And it wasn't just his physical prowess or artful bed play, but something more. Something—intangible. A ferocious yet tender protectiveness.

She shook away the silliness of her musings and reached for the platter of bread, cheese, slices of apple, and raspberries. The sweet tartness of the fruit tamed the sharpness of the pale cheese she recognized as coming from the nearest village. The bread was tough but edible. It could be worse. At least they hadn't left her a bowl of those boiled oats Scots seemed to love so much.

As she finished the ale, a familiar voice caught her attention. Deep. Rumbling. She smiled. There was her Scottish bear. He spoke with someone just past the entrance of the tent. She rose quietly, edging forward with her head inclined to catch every word.

"It was Marta," said a voice she didn't recognize. "Naked. Staked to the cliff." The speaker paused and made a noise that sounded like a cross between a gag and a cough. "Scavengers had already got to her."

"But ye recovered what was left of her?" Thorburn asked.

"Aye. They're taking her to Craignure now. They'll see her buried proper."

"Ensure they know it was not done by my order," Thorburn advised. "I dinna mind them fearing us, but I willna have them thinking we stoop to such cowardly acts as feeding old women to the terns."

"I shall see to it, Constable."

Adellis knew very well who had ordered such a thing done to the healer. Alrek thrived on such cruelties and used them to maintain a high level of fear and obedience among his servants. She retreated a step as Thorburn entered the tent.

"Good morning to ye, m'lady." His swaggering gait revealed no limp or soreness in his injured leg.

"Good morning." She nodded toward his knee. "It appears that whisky, honey, and vigorous exercise have healed you."

His smile reflected the same devilment dancing in his eyes. "Aye, m'lady. Ye worked wonders for me." His gaze traveled across her like a lover's caress. "And how are ye this morning? Yer wound? Is it better?"

Without hesitating, she lifted her tunic and exposed her hip. She peeled away the bandage and smiled. The gash looked a great deal less angry and well on its way to mending. "It appears the treatment benefited me as well." She warmed her tone with seductive invitation. She wanted him. Again. Now. "We should administer more tonic. Do you not agree?"

His demeanor immediately changed. With his chin slanting to a determined angle, he resettled his stance. The muscles in his throat and jaw flexed with a hard swallow. "I do agree. Most wholeheartedly," he said, but instead of coming to her, shifted his focus to the table beside them. With a sweep of his hand, he motioned to a stool. "However—I feel it important we talk first. Yer seat, m'lady."

Experience had taught her the canniness to control her composure and keep her uneasiness hidden. She gave a regal nod of acceptance, then lowered herself to the seat and folded her hands on the table. "And what shall we speak of, my bear? I shared *everything* with you last night." She could tell by the way the corners of his eyes tightened, then relaxed that he read her meaning.

He didn't answer right away. Instead, he seated himself opposite her, on the side toward the exit. Was he still so leery of her? After everything they had shared? She accepted the leeriness as a compliment. The twined joints of his stool creaked beneath his weight. Scowling, he looked down and wiggled. "Hendry should see to this one."

Her mighty Scot was stalling. Uncomfortable about something. The tensed angle of his shoulders and fisted hand on the table betrayed him. Never one to play about with words, she leaned forward with the same cold ferocity that made her brother's meeker followers avoid her. "Speak your fears, lest they control you."

"Marta is dead. Found staked to a cliff."

"I heard." She felt no reason to conceal her eavesdropping. At least, not this time. "I can promise you her end was ordered by my brother."

"I need to understand why ye havena escaped him before now?" He squared himself up to the table and rested both massive forearms in front of him. "Ye proved yerself a powerful warrior. Cunning as a wee fox. I am certain ye've resources of yer own, being the sister to the jarl and all. I fail to see how ye couldna distance yerself from that fool before now." His gaze slid to the stake where she had been chained. "And in a less dangerous way than allowing yerself to be taken prisoner."

"That is because you are a man," she said with a sharpness she regretted. She must not allow him to goad her into losing control and revealing anything she didn't wish shared. Some things, some memories, were better left undisturbed. While she would always be honest with him, that didn't mean she had to tell him everything.

"I have known women in Norway to own property. Manage their own households. Survive without the benefit of a man. How is it ye say ye couldna be free?"

"Do not judge me when you know nothing of what I have lived." A surprising disappointment filled her. The *Gallóglaigh* Constable had shown himself to be a typical man, after all. He appeared either unable or unwilling to understand the difficulty of escaping the clutches of a madman who had charmed and intimidated an entire clan into following him. So be it. She hadn't expected him to understand, and it was just as well. Knowing this would make leaving him easier once they reached Scotland.

"I would like water for washing," she said, considering the subject closed.

"Not until ye tell me what ye have endured, so I might understand ye better."

"Why is it so important you understand me? I told you enough last night."

"Because I canna fully trust ye if I dinna understand ye, and if I dinna trust ye, I canna help ye." He cast a glance back over his shoulder and shouted, "Hendry! Ale."

The boy appeared before the echo of his liege's shout had fully faded. He placed two tankards and a pitcher on the table, then gave her a shy bob of his head. "Good morning to ye, m'lady. If the clothes I gathered dinna suit ye, I can find others that might. Just tell me what ye need."

"Thank you, Hendry." As long as the garb covered her and didn't interfere with self-defense, she didn't care if it looked comely. But she wouldn't tell Hendry that. Not when it seemed so important to him. "I appreciate your kindness." She graced him with a genuine smile. "Some water for washing would be nice."

"Aye, m'lady. I shall set the water to heating." The lad dipped his tousled head again, then rushed back outside.

Thorburn slid her tankard closer. "Now, help me understand ye, Adellis. I can better help ye if I understand and know ye trust me, as well."

He wished to hear her truths? Fine. She would tell him what she could bear to bring into the light. The cool metal of the tankard centered her as she cupped her hands around it and stared down at her reflection. "Alrek arranged the death of our father." That was one of her brighter memories. A time of relief and hope that life might change and improve. She ran her thumb along the mug's handle. "I paid a share of the silver because our sire was a cruel man. Often crazed with fits of unreasonable anger. His murder won Alrek the allegiance of most in the clan." A bitter laugh escaped her. "But it appears the tendency toward barbaric madness passed from father to son."

Thorburn didn't speak nor drink from his cup. Just sat there. Silent. Watching her.

Her shoulder twitched as if her body rebelled about reliving what came next. "After claiming the jarldom, Alrek took it upon himself to arrange a marriage for me. A union that would ensure him powerful allies, additional lands, and money. When I refused, he had me tied to a post and whipped in front of the clan because I had chosen my own wishes over their well-being. Or so he said." The horror came back to her as if it had happened yesterday. In fact, she relived it every night in her dreams. The unholy gleam in her brother's eyes as he had watched the torture.

The demons in her dreams had her brother's eyes. Even though they had shared their mother's womb, he had always hated her, and she had never known why. All she knew for certain, for as far back as she could remember, was she hated him, too.

"Once I healed and regained my strength, I ran away." She tensed at the memory of that terrible failure. "They tracked me to the village where I took refuge, tied me to the common well, then barricaded everyone inside their houses and set fire to everything." She took a long, deep drink, then clunked the tankard back onto the table. "I still hear the screams of those who helped me whenever I see a red sunset."

Without a word, Thorburn refilled her tankard. He made as though to speak, but she held up a hand and stopped him. "I am not finished, my inquisitive bear." After a deep breath, she continued. "After that, I thought ridding myself of my virginity would solve Alrek bartering it away. Taking lovers protected me somewhat." She shrugged. "At least until my brother started killing them off. Men are not so lusty when they fear death."

"How came ye to be a warrior?" he asked quietly. "How did ye convince yer brother to allow that?"

She stared off into the distance, remembering back to the day that fate had finally helped her. "I used his ego and madness against him." Satisfaction at that one success tickled the corner of her mouth. "And a bit of heather ale I brewed with the help of our seer before she died."

"Heather ale?" Confusion furrowed Thorburn's brow.

"Heather and an herb the seer wouldn't tell me the name of steeped in a kettle of Alrek's favorite port. She told me to trust her." A sigh escaped her. "I did. She and my mother were the only ones left in the clan I knew I could trust."

"So, how did this heather ale work such magic and make him grant ye a sword?"

"We offered the brew to Alrek with the promise that if he was truly descended from Vikings, it would mix with his blood and give him visions. Divine whisperings from the gods themselves." She rubbed the long, thin scar on the inside of her left wrist. The scar she had gotten the night she had given Alrek the drink. A good portion of blood had also been required for the potion.

"The brew turned him into a blubbering fool at first. But the seer told me not to worry and bade me *suggest*, to plant the seed of what I wished into his mind. So, I planted my desire for freedom, and just in case he was more coherent than he acted, I seeded the wish to fight at his side with the ferocity of the fabled Valkyrie. I chose my wording carefully. Alrek might be insane, but he is dangerously sly." She shook herself free of the past and leveled her gaze with Thorburn's. "My wish to fight appeared to be the only seed that took root before the drink sent him screaming into the darkness. I thought him poisoned for certain. Hoped for it, even. But he lived."

"Why did ye not just kill him?" He still doubted her. She could see it in his eyes.

"A canny coward keeps himself well guarded at all times. Alrek has a legion of personal guards." She paused to fill their tankards again. "And he always made certain to remind me that Mother was in the tower and would suffer even more if he died. He had a standing order that she be skinned alive and staked out for the ravens should any ill befall him."

"His own mother? Yer mother?" he repeated in a hushed voice.

"Yes." She hadn't planned to share that part, but somehow, it just rolled off her tongue. "After I had foiled his efforts any way I could, he imprisoned our mother in the tower with the promise that if I refused his will one more time, she would suffer for it." Her eyes stung, but it couldn't be tears. She had given up weeping long ago. Tears changed nothing. "Mother hanged herself with her belt. I found her. Along with a letter containing her blessing and the hope that her death would grant me the freedom I deserved. She also begged my forgiveness. For everything." She blinked away the vision forever burned into her mind. After draining her mug, she clunked it back to the table. "That was the day before we set sail for Mull."

He stared down at his drink, scowling into the tankard, one finger tapping against its side. "So ye thought then to allow yerself captured by *Gallóglaigh* to escape him?"

"Yes."

"Ye realize ye couldha been killed or worse?" A sternness tightened Thorburn's mouth. He thumped the table, then bounced his fist off his chest. "Not all captors are as benevolent toward women as myself, ye ken? What if a darker fate had befallen ye?"

"I have endured *darker* and was prepared for it." He did not know her trials. Life had tempered her with unforgiving fire. She was as hard as the finest steel and proud of it. "Capture was my surest way of escape, endangering no one other than myself." She locked eyes with him, willing him to understand and believe. "Too many have suffered and died because of me."

"I still canna see why ye didna kill the bastard yerself? Yer a canny lass. Ye couldha found a way."

"Before her imprisonment, my mother made me swear to never kill him." Of that, she would say no more. Mother always blamed herself for Alrek's twisted mind, but Adellis never knew why. The reason was made clear in the letter Mother left behind. Adellis had always suspected after picking up on some rumors. But she never knew for certain until she read the words in Mother's own hand. How Father forced her to choose which child she would surrender to Father's allies whenever they visited. Rich, titled men with an illicit hunger for the young and helpless.

She straightened her spine, waiting for her Scottish bear's next argument. After all, experience taught her that men never believed a woman's trials and tribulations. When he didn't speak, she rose from the stool, hiked her tunic up around her neck, and turned her back to him. "To help you believe my words, here is my witness in the harsh light of day—the soft touch of the candles hid my proof last night."

A hissing sound, the sharp intake of air through clenched teeth filled the tent.

As the shirt fell back in place, she faced him. "And now, Master Constable, might I have the water for washing?"

Jaw tight and hard, he rose and strode over to the stake. With a mighty pull, he tore it free of the ground and hurled it into the corner. Gaze locked on the doorway, he slanted a polite bow in her direction. "Ye will be provided with whatever ye wish, m'lady."

Then he charged outside without looking back.

CHAPTER FIVE

"Ye no longer consider her a spoil of war then?" Ross scowled at Thorburn, his tone raging like thunder. The retelling of Adellis's tale had resurrected dangerous memories and all the emotions that came with them.

"Nor a prisoner." Valan glowered at them both, just as furious as his brother.

"That is correct," Thorburn confirmed. "She is my protected guest."

"And how do ye intend to explain her to the MacDougall?" Ross shifted his attention to the men in the makeshift practice yard in the meadow beside the tents. With his hardened scowl locked on the sparring men, he added, "Ye ken several witnessed the stripping away of her armor and even more watched ye carry her into yer quarters and order her staked there."

"And the knaves are a chatter about the warrior beauty captured by the constable," Valan shared before charging toward a pair of men not wielding their sparths properly. "What the hell is that?" he boomed. "Who taught ye to hold yer axe in that manner?"

"The MacDougall is a fair man," Thorburn reasoned more to himself than Ross. Even though his gaze remained locked on Valan thrashing the two sluggards, his mind wandered back to his tent. He focused on Adellis and all they had shared. "Surely, our liege will grant her sanctuary once he hears of all she has endured."

But even though he spoke the reassurance aloud, he feared it might prove false. While the MacDougall *was* an honorable man, his people viewed him with a healthy dose of fear added to their respect. The Lord of Argyll ruled with unyielding ferocity. He tolerated no bending or loose interpretations of his edicts. The man would be sore pressed to give a Norwegian refuge. He hated them for all they had cost the clan.

"The chore will be convincing him to let her live long enough to tell her tale." Ross frowned at another pair of men bashing each other with shields and maces. "He's had his fill of the delays at Duart. Wants the castle built and done, so we can be sent elsewhere for more profit. He knows it's the Northmen stirring the villagers and making them fearful." With a side-eyed glance, he gave a doubtful shrug. "And it appears to be the brother of our lovely guest causing all the trouble." Ross turned to deliver a more pointed glare. "If all she says is true."

"I saw her scars." Last night, during their bed play, Thorburn had vaguely noticed an odd texture to the skin across her back, but he had been so inflamed with lust, he'd paid it no mind. But this morning, when she bared herself and revealed the proof of the flaying, any doubts about her story disappeared. The memory of it sickened him. That woman possessed a strength few men could claim, and at that moment, he had sworn to help her, no matter what it took.

"We should capture her brother and give him a taste of the same." Ross clapped him on the shoulder, then went still. Both his brows climbed to his hairline as he stared at something behind them. "Who gave her those clothes?"

Thorburn turned and fell just as still as Ross. "Hendry." The artless young knave had misjudged the lady's sizing. Or maybe not. Perhaps wee Hendry appreciated the female form more than he let on. The trews he had found fit the lass like a second skin, revealing the shapeliness of her long, muscular legs. The fresh léine was less full than her own and only reached to her crotch.

Dark blue and belted, she wore the neckline untied, and the snug sleeves rolled partway up her forearms. Tasgall had returned her knee-high boots to her, but thankfully, the lethal heel spikes had been removed. Striding forward with her silvery hair caught back in braids, she resembled the Valkyrie she had spoken of, ready and able to whisk his deserving warriors away to Valhalla.

"I would practice with your men," she announced with a disarming smile as she joined them.

"That willna be allowed." He stared at her, trying to decide if she had said it in jest. Surely she had. "Why would ye wish to do such a thing?"

"I shall leave the two of ye to discuss this." Ross offered a polite nod. "M'lady." He gave Thorburn an irritatingly smug smile. "Brother."

"The three of you look the same," she said as her gaze followed Ross, slid to Valan, then returned to him. "Great blonde bears. Your father must be proud." She selected a spear from the rack and hefted it in one hand.

Thorburn took the spear from her and put it back in the rack. "He was. Verra proud." With as gentle a firmness as he could muster, he turned her away from the array of weapons. "I discussed yer plight with my brothers. Ye are now my protected guest." He proffered a stern nod. "And my guests dinna spar with my men."

One of her pale brows rose as she loosely folded her arms across her middle. "While I appreciate the elevation to the level of guest, I must practice to maintain my skills." A faint smile teased the corner of her mouth. "I realize you are the legendary *Gallóglaigh,* but my brother's forces are just as lethal. I must be ready when he comes for me. My safety does not fall to you alone."

A strong surge of protectiveness washed across him, along with the sting of her lack of confidence in himself and his men. He moved closer and touched her cheek, cupping her face in his palm. "I promise ye, m'lady. Ye are safe with me."

"Do not make promises you cannot keep," she said softly, brushing her fingertips across the back of his hand.

Her hair reflected the brilliance of the morning's sunlight, giving her the mesmerizing glow of an angel. He swallowed hard as he watched escaped wisps dancing in the breeze, framing the curves of her features like an ethereal halo. He sensed a vulnerability about her, an untapped gentleness. The realization unleashed a raging torrent of emotions within him, tightening every muscle and sinew. What this warrior princess didn't realize was that he had never been one to share anything. Once he claimed something and swore to protect it, all others had best leave it alone. She belonged to him and would do well to learn that. "No one takes what is mine, m'lady. Not ever. Ye will be safe."

She stared up at him, her sweet lips barely parted. He caught a glimpse of her surprise before her iron-willed control whisked it back into hiding.

"I am not yours," she corrected matter-of-factly.

"Aye, m'lady. Ye are, for I have claimed ye." He bent his head and took her mouth with his, not giving a damn that the noise of his men sparring in the adjoining field went quiet.

Her breath hitched, but she leaned into him, sealing the bond with a proper return of fiery heat. The weight of her hand rested in the center of his chest, right above his heart. Aye, she was his. At least for as long as she allowed it. He lifted his head and smiled down at her. She looked flustered for the first time since her capture, and it suited her. What a rare woman she was.

"Constable!"

The interruption made him growl. He turned to seek the owner of the shout and immediately tensed. Edrid, a man better than a dog on the hunt when it came to sniffing out secrets, limped toward him with blood streaming down the side of his face and an arm clutched across his middle. "What happened to ye, man?"

"Northmen." He winced as he wheezed in a gasp of air. "East

of here past the ridge." He bent and spit out a mouthful of blood, keeping himself upright with one hand propped on his knee. With a painful whistling sound, he struggled to draw in enough air to speak. "More than last time, but not all Norse. I think I recognized some from Craignure."

"He promises the villagers aid from Norway," Adellis said. She stepped up to the man and examined his head wound. "Empty offers of silver. More land. Goods. Trading." She slowly shook her head. "Alrek tells them whatever they wish to hear." She lightly rested her hand on the arm Edrid held locked across his body. Bending closer, she forced him to look her in the eyes. "Is it your arm or your ribs you protect? Which is hurt?"

"Ribs," the spy hissed through clenched teeth. "I canna breathe since one of the buggers caught me with his feckin' club." He tried to pull away, but she held fast, holding him in place as she checked him over. With a frustrated look at Thorburn, he tipped his head in her direction. "I thought she was yer prisoner?"

"Not any longer." He wouldn't go into details with Edrid. More important matters demanded his attention now. "I suppose they are moving on to Duart to tear down what's been rebuilt after their last treachery?"

"Aye." Edrid spit out more blood.

Her mouth a tight, stern line, Adellis stepped back. "The head wound is not severe. Merely needs cleaning." Then her expression became pained. "But the blood he spits is worrisome. He is hurt inside. We can do nothing for the broken ribs other than bandage them. If either of your knaves have any sage or thorn apple, the smoke might ease him some. Help him breathe. Other than that, nothing will aid him but rest." She shrugged. "And whisky for the pain."

"Hendry will help ye tend him." He motioned toward the camp. "To my tent with ye, Edrid. Ye're a valuable man. I canna have ye out of commission for any length of time."

"Thank ye, my constable." The man gave a respectful nod, then limped away.

Before Adellis followed, Thorburn caught hold of her arm. "I thank ye for tending him while we go to meet yer brother in battle."

She frowned. "I will tell Hendry what to do, but then I shall come with you. Or follow if ye must leave now."

"Come with us?"

"Of course." She squinted toward the east, shielding her eyes from the sun. "I can help. I know Alrek's tactics." With a proud upward jut of her chin, she added, "And I can fight. You know that."

He shook his head. "Out of the question." Frustration mounting, he pointed at his tent. "When ye came under my protection, ye also came under my word. Ye will do as yer told, m'lady. To the tent with ye. Now. To stay."

"I will do as I will," she informed him in a low growl. His warrior princess's fire had returned in all its glory. "I did not escape one keeper to become imprisoned by another."

"It was yer choice," he said in a voice louder than he meant to use. How she could she be so unwise as well as so ungrateful? "Ye wished capture to escape yer bastard of a brother, and now it is done. Ye are now under my rule, m'lady. Get thee to the tent and be thankful for it, ye ken?"

"I will not take orders from a bloody Scot!"

God's beard! Was he going to have to have her chained again? He scrubbed a hand down his face, wondering which of his sins had cursed him with being tempted by such a stubborn wee hellcat—and how in blazes could she still be so bloody enticing even while angering him beyond reason?

"Has it not occurred to ye that ye would be safer here in camp?" When she didn't answer, he gritted his teeth to keep from roaring. No one disobeyed his orders. Not ever. "In the thick of battle, ye could be reclaimed without us knowing until it was too late. Did ye not think of that, my thick-headed beauty?" That won him an angry tightening of her eyes, but at least the hard set of her jaw appeared to soften the slightest bit. Perhaps his reasoning was finally worming its way through her wall of unyielding bullheadedness. "I understand ye could never depend on anyone other than yerself before, but I swear, ye can depend on me now."

"Why?" She spit the word at him, but her tone wasn't as sharp.

"Because I admire ye. Surely, ye know that." How could the woman be so blind? "And I am drawn to ye, damn ye. I want more time at yer side." He flipped a hand as though swatting at his fumbling words. "I am nay just speaking about ye warming my bed, but time to know yer ways and learn how ye think."

She didn't answer nor reveal the workings of her mind, just maintained her infuriating silence and icy glare.

The ease with which she riled him struck something akin to fear deep in his soul. He stabbed a finger into the air again and shook it at her. "Or maybe it's because ye've bewitched me into being a foolhardy eedjit. How the hell do I know why I wish for ye to depend on me? Just be thankful I do, ye ken?"

Her icy demeanor melted, warmed by a faint smile. After a mocking curtsy, she inclined her head. "By your leave then, Constable." She spun and strode away, the mouthwatering sway of her comely hips reminding him to speak to Hendry about finding her some proper clothing that would be a mite more modest.

His fists tightened until every knuckle popped. This woman would be the death of him. He felt certain of it.

"HE NEEDS A cloth draped over his head whilst he leans over the bowl. The steam must surround him, so he breathes it in." She decided against burning the herbs and having the man breathe in the smoke. It could make him cough, and that would be excruciating with those broken ribs. But inhaling the warm steam as the herbs steeped in the hot water might ease him well enough. At least, she hoped so.

He had ceased spitting blood, but his color had gone a disturbing gray. The longer she watched him, the more she feared it didn't really matter what they did for the poor man. The ultimate outcome would be the same. She wondered if Thorburn carried the bodies of his dead back to Scotland or buried them on Mull. Alrek always dumped his into the sea, no matter what their family wished. No fine Viking funeral. Not even any words said over the bodies before he tossed them out. Alrek reveled in heartless disrespect. Considered it a strength of leadership.

"Here is a linen, m'lady." Hendry's expression revealed he possessed the same worries about Edrid.

"If you can bear sitting up for a few good breaths, then Hendry and I will help you to the pallet so you might rest."

Elbows on the table and head propped in his hands, Edrid didn't bother looking up. "I can bear it a while longer."

Adellis had her doubts. The man's trembling revealed he held himself upright by will alone.

"M'lord asks that ye come outside, m'lady," Tasgall said as he rushed into the tent. He stowed metalworking tools and weapons into the leather tote he carried into battle for Thorburn. "We be leaving within the hour, so he bids ye make haste."

"Stay at his side," she whispered to Hendry with a pointed look.

The lad gave her a nod, assuring he understood she didn't wish the poor man to die alone.

Wiping her hands on the cloth tied around her waist, she hurried outside to find Thorburn. He stood contemplating a shield that looked the worse for wear.

"Retire that one," she advised, still drying her hands on the apron.

"She might have another battle left in her." He slid his hand through the grip and hefted it to waist level. "See?"

With a running spin, she landed a hard kick against the upper half of the disc and splintered off the top two sections of the wood. The metal banding holding the boards in place bent over Thorburn's arm. "There. She has fought her last battle. Now cast it aside and choose one that will properly protect you."

"Is it yer life's joy to prove me wrong?" He peeled off the broken shield and threw it to the ground beside the fire.

"It is becoming such." Perturbing him did bring her joy. That fuming glint in his eyes filled her heart with a happiness unlike any other. Such a rare feeling, one that gave her a satisfying warmness. "I do not wish you injured, my bear. You are my protection, remember?" When his lopsided grin deepened his dimple, she knew he had forgiven the slight to his ego.

"Ten of my best shall remain here to guard ye, m'lady." He selected another shield and held it up. "Does this one meet with yer approval?"

"Yes," she answered even though she hadn't taken her gaze from his. The emotions playing across his face sculpted a shadow she feared to decipher. "That one is fine."

"Ye didna even look," he gently chided.

"I looked," she said, not meaning the shield, but the thoughts reflected in his eyes. "My brother always fights at the back like the coward he is. Watch for him there." She moved closer, drawn by that strange force her Scottish bear possessed. She couldn't explain or resist his subtle, unspoken invitation. "Alrek looks like me. But bigger." A knowing smile tickled her mouth. Her mighty Thor's stature made her smile. "But Alrek is not nearly as powerful as you, my fine protector."

He met her halfway and pulled her to his chest. "The thought of returning to you, of holding you again, will render me invincible." Resting his cheek atop her head, his arms tightened around her. "Shall I bring ye the bastard's head on a platter?"

Even though she heard his every word, she found herself unable to speak. Something about his manner, his choice of wording. He spoke not like the useful lover and manner of transportation she intended him to be, but as one filled with kindness, one who truly cared about her wellbeing.

"Adellis?"

"Yes?" she whispered, frightened at the revelation. To care brought nothing but danger and pain. Loss always followed caring.

"Forgive me if I upset ye." He eased her back, holding her at arms' length. "I reckon ye still care about him. After all, he is yer brother."

"We shared our mother's womb, our father's blood, and a hatred for one another." She found herself filled with unreasonable fear. The fear of once again being left alone and cast adrift, the fear of again losing someone she could someday care about. "All I wish for you to bring me is yourself. Safe and whole. Alrek is crazed but sly as a stoat and fights with every level of evil he possesses. Do not underestimate him."

She could tell by the set of his mouth that he was as uneasy about this closeness as she was. He was a warrior. A mercenary. Her Scottish bear had no use for entanglements in his life. At least not for the long term. "Promise me you will not underestimate him. Your Lord of Argyll will not look kindly upon me if my brother kills the commander of his forces." There. That should ease his worries and make him know that her only concern was her freedom. Then he would rest assured that as soon as possible, he would be free of her, too. A sorrowful pang squeezed her heart, but she did her best to ignore it. *He will be free of me*, she repeated to herself. That was how it had to be.

"If I fall, my brothers will take care of ye. I have spoken to them."

"I am grateful." The gentle way he touched her face made her want to sob—and she hadn't sobbed for anyone in a very long while.

"I willna fall," he whispered as he leaned in for a kiss. "Dinna fash yerself, m'love."

She dodged him and framed his face between her hands. "I will never forgive you if you fall. I will think you a liar." When he tried to claim the kiss, she stopped him again. "And never call me 'm'love' again. For that will never happen between us. Do you understand me?"

He frowned. "Dinna fear, I willna place any obligations upon ye, lass. I understand yer need for complete freedom." His head tilted enough to make his blonde warrior's braid slide across his shoulder as he studied her. "Ye and I are verra much alike. I see no harm in a friendship and our enjoyment of one another's company."

Even though she heartily agreed, a vague disappointment, a sense of an opportunity lost squeezed her heart again. "Friendship," she repeated. "That is all."

"Aye, love," he said in a rasping whisper as he held her tighter. "We two shall be verra good friends. Mark my word, ye ken?"

She silenced him by surrendering to his need for a kiss and to her own ravenous urge to taste him one last time before he charged into battle. The inexplicable yearning to follow him, to protect him from harm, made her cling tighter, prevent him from leaving without her. This man might be a fearsome warrior, but he was still just a man. Able to bleed. To suffer. To die. When he pulled away and stared down at her, he knew what she felt, what she feared; she could see the reflection of it in his eyes.

"If ye came, I wouldna fight as well. A victorious warrior must remain focused on the enemy—not fretting about..."

The way his words tapered off made her swallow hard and take a step back. The worrisome aching in her chest pounded harder, making her wish she could claw it away and escape the troublesome feelings. She hated to feel. It made her vulnerable.

"I will remain here as you wish." She coughed away the tremor in her voice. With a glance back at the tent, she stood taller, prouder, colder. "I fear your man will leave this world soon. What do you do with your dead? I will see to it whilst you are away."

Thorburn's intense stare turned into a scowl. "We take our dead home to their families. Hendry knows how to prepare the bodies."

All that was left unsaid between them charged the air until it threatened to crackle like lightning. Without another word, Thorburn gave a jerking nod, scooped up his shield, and stormed away. After several long strides, he halted and bowed his head as though about to steal a glance back at her and speak. But he didn't. Instead, he lifted his head, stared forward, and charged on.

Such a man, her Scottish bear. She hoped he fought the same way he loved, with every fiber of his being.

"M'lady?"

The uncomfortable pinch to Hendry's voice told her Edrid had found his peace. The lad's pallor made her realize that perhaps Thorburn had overestimated this knave's knowledge about caring for the dead. "Do you have the balms to prepare him for his journey?" She already knew the answer by the panicked rounding of the boy's eyes. "Your master spoke as though you knew what to do," she gently chided.

"The *Gallóglaigh* rarely die," Hendry whispered with a backward glance at the entrance to the tent. "At least, none have since I started serving the constable."

"All men die, Hendry," she said as she marched inside. She knelt down and held her hand beneath the spy's nose to ensure he had died and wasn't just unconscious from his pain. No air stirred against her skin, and the cooling down of his now waxy flesh confirmed that the unnerved boy had at least gotten that part right. The man was dead.

She rose from the floor, trying to remember what the old wise woman of the clan had done for the dead. As near as she could remember, the body needed to be washed with the best heated white wine on hand, massaged with resin, then a combination of herbs had to be stuffed down the man's throat and up his nose. Since Hendry appeared to be at a loss, she made up her mind to do what she had done most of her life. Do what felt right, then live with the results. She counted off on her fingers, "Set some white wine to heating. Add to it cloves and whatever other strong-smelling herbs you have on hand. Oakum, myrrh, incense of any kind."

"Garlic?"

"No." At least, she didn't think so. She couldn't remember the smell of garlic during any funeral rites. "Do you have balsam and enough linen to wrap his body?"

The knave gave her a hesitant shrug. "Linens, I have. Balsam?" He shook his head. "I dinna think we have any resin at all."

"We have to find some kind of resin to mix with more of the myrrh." Adellis frowned down at the body, wondering what trees on the Isle of Mull might prove helpful in the preservation of the dead.

"I have plenty of myrrh." The boy opened a trunk, revealing a cornucopia of jars, crocks, and bottles, carefully fitted into wood-slatted frames to keep them safe during transport. He lifted up a corked jar filled with chunks of golden-brown nuggets. "If we mix it with oil, will that not be enough resin?"

"Our wise woman always used balsam and myrrh. It preserves the body longer." Another casual glance around the opulent tent made her realize the camp didn't appear all that temporary. How long had they planned on staying here? With it being summer, the deceased wouldn't keep overlong before becoming very unpleasant. "When did your master plan on returning to Scotland?"

Hendry gave her a fiercely proud glare. "M'lord leaves nothing unfinished. He's sworn not to leave until the head of the vile Northman responsible for all the troubles is on a pike in front of his tent."

Adellis curled her nose at the prospect of keeping the body for however long that might take. Alrek would not be vanquished with ease. "We should prepare Edrid as best we can, then send him on to Duart for transport back to Scotland on the next ship. Surely, they can place him in a casket at Duart." She twitched her nose again. "Trust me, it will be better that way."

With a doubtful tip of his head, Hendry bent to select herbs and oils from the chest and set them on the table. "No one leaves camp while the constable is away. We can do what we must for poor Edrid, but we must keep him here until everyone returns to bid him a proper farewell."

"Give me a crock and a knife," she said, deciding not to waste her time arguing about when the fallen man should go to the port beyond the castle.

"What do ye wish with a crock and a knife?"

"I intend to find some sort of resin for us to mix with the myrrh." When he didn't move, she added, "I am not fond of the stench of decaying flesh. Are you?"

Hendry gagged and fixed an accusing glare at the man on the floor. "I wish he hadna died."

"I agree it was very inconsiderate of him." Rather than wait on Hendry, she fetched one of the woven bags off a peg and helped herself to a small empty jar and a curved knife sheathed in the lid of the spice trunk. "Drag him outside while I'm gone. It's best we prepare him somewhere other than here in your master's tent." She started toward the door, then stopped. "But be sure and put him in the shade."

"Ye shouldna go alone." Hendry hefted the deceased up by the armpits, huffing and grunting as he attempted to inch the body across the floor. The boy acted as if it weighed more than an ox.

"How did you survive before becoming a knave?" She nudged the lad aside, caught up the corners of the fur beneath the bulk of the man's body, and dragged it backward out of the tent.

"By my wits," he huffed as he took hold of the fur beside the man's ankles and helped her shift the body well beneath the trees into the deep shade. As he straightened, he gave her an insulted look that made her feel as though she had behaved with as much heartlessness as her brother always did. "I know I will never be a warrior, but I see that m'lord receives nothing but the best and doesna want for a thing in this hard but honorable path he has chosen to follow."

"Forgive me, Hendry. I should not have spoken so callously." She patted the bag slung across her body, rattling the knife against the earthenware jar within. "I shall not be gone long. Set the wine to heating, and be sure and add every herb you can find that has a stout yet pleasing scent. Flowers, too, if you can find them."

"It isna right that ye leave camp with no one to protect ye. Let me call one of the men. M'lord made it verra clear that we were to remain on our guard at all times."

All she intended to do was scrape some trees in search of sap to mix with the myrrh. What harm could come to her? "I promise to remain right over there." She pointed deeper into the cluster of trees shading this side of the camp. "In this area here. Close. In fact, you should be able to hear me while you work at the fire. If it will calm you, I shall talk to you while I am among the trees, so you know no ill has befallen me."

He gave her a dubious wrinkling of his nose.

"I am going whether you will it or not." She hoped she wouldn't have to hurt the lad's feelings by showing how he couldn't stop her even if he tried his best. Without another word, she stepped between the trees, wishing she had paid more attention when the healer had tried to teach her herbal lore.

"Ye said ye would talk," came the knave's nervous call.

"I am right here, Hendry." She fingered a tender young sapling, then called out, "What about willow bark? Do you think that might work?"

"I fear he is beyond that, m'lady. It relieves pain, and I dinna think much anything troubles him anymore."

"Fair point," she muttered, realizing her error as soon as the boy said it. The healer had scolded her often for not paying attention and trying to remember more.

"What did ye say?"

"Nothing," she called back, tromping deeper into the woods. What she needed was a good sturdy fir or pine. That would give them some stout pitch.

"Where are ye now, m'lady?"

"Right here. Is the wine boiling yet?" Hendry was as worrisome as a buzzing midge.

A hand clamped over her mouth and slammed her back against an armored chest. Sharp spikes stabbed into the flesh from the base of her neck to the small of her back. A sickening dizziness fouled her senses as the poisoned barbs dove deeper with the fiend's tightening embrace. Her last coherent feeling was hopelessness. She had erred so badly. Her chance at freedom was gone. But even worse, she would never see her fearsome Scottish bear ever again. Nor would she be able to admit she liked it when he called her *m'love*.

CHAPTER SIX

"I SEE NO sign of them. Anywhere." Perched on the crumbling edge of a tall crag, Thorburn scanned the landscape.

"Edrid never errs," Ross said, frowning down at the gently rolling land stretching between their current position and the point reaching out into the sea where the construction of Duart Castle sent up columns of smoke from the workers' fires.

Thorburn backed away from the cliff's edge, thinking back over all the spy had told him. Edrid spoke as if he had witnessed a large group of marauders heading for Duart before one of them bashed him with a club. And that was the part that didn't make sense. Why did they not finish the job and kill the man? Or torture him for information? From all Adellis had told him, and from the proof of the scars on her back, her brother thrived on tormenting prisoners. Why had they allowed Edrid to escape, knowing he would report not only their position but their numbers?

An eerie knowing made him turn and stare back at where they had just been. What Edrid had reported was nothing more than a diversion. Carefully laid bait to lure them away from camp, and Thorburn knew why. Teeth clenched so hard his jaws ached, he bowed his head. He prayed those he had left behind managed to hold off however many dogs Jarl Alrek had sent to fetch his sister.

"A trap?" Ross asked.

"Aye, a feckin' snare for sure." Thorburn lifted his head, regret and anger surging through him at a slow burn. They had made a fool of him. "I shouldha allowed her to come with us. That wouldha foiled the bastard's plans. Instead, I did exactly as he guessed I would and left her there. Like a lamb staked out for wolves."

Without a word, Ross gave the signal to turn about. It rippled through the twoscore of men awaiting their orders. The unit shifted and turned as one. With an apologetic tip of his head, Ross glanced skyward. "It will take us 'til nightfall to get back, ye ken?"

"I am well aware of that." Thorburn charged down the incline. "Tasgall!"

"Aye, m'lord?"

"Off with it. All of it." He tossed his helm to the ground and yanked loose his belt. "And rid my horse of any extra weight. I need a mount unencumbered and fast. Make haste, ye ken?" Bending forward, he hunched the heavy shirt of mail up to his shoulders.

"Aye, m'lord." The knave finished the job and dragged the hauberk off him. Tasgall scooped up the helmet, then placed the articles onto his own steed, lashing them behind the saddle. "Ye'll be keeping yer axe, aye? And the dagger?"

"Aye." Stripped down to nothing but his trews and léine, Thorburn belted his dagger to his side and placed his massive sparth into the specially fashioned leather holder attached to his saddle. He tossed the shield to Tasgall, then launched himself onto his mount. Lighter meant faster, and he needed swiftness more than ever before. Praise God, they had ridden rather than marched to intercept the troublemakers before they reached Duart. They usually preferred tracking foes on foot. But a hasty pace had been foremost this time. Now he could speedily retrace their path. Unfortunately, even at a mighty gallop, it would take 'til nearly nightfall to make it back.

"Lead them, Ross," he shouted over his shoulder as he spurred the horse onward. Both Ross and Valan had led the guard before. In fact, if he had failed at assuming command, the position of constable would have fallen to one of his brothers. Their father had led the *Gallóglaigh* until his death, and his father before that. To lead was expected of them. It was the heritage of their bloodline.

He kept close to the coastline at first, maneuvering around the wet spongy patches of blanket bog and tangles of heath. That terrain slowed him too much, forcing him to veer inland to the grasslands. Rippling thatches of green fescue and bright pink sea thrift provided somewhat easier traveling, but it still wasn't fast enough to suit him. God's beard, he wished he could sprout the wings of an eagle and soar to whatever awaited.

A column of dark smoke staining the vibrant blue of the sky squeezed the air from his lungs. Just as he feared. A sprung trap. The cowardly bastard had burned them out. His warriors could do little against flaming arrows shot from carefully chosen vantage points. He pushed his mount harder, even though the beast already foamed at the mouth. As he thundered closer, the rumbling of chaos and enraged shouting reached him. His men's anger roared louder than the crackling blaze engulfing the encampment.

He leapt from the saddle and charged into the heart of it. Most of the shelters were gone, their remains nothing more than patches of smoldering blackness, glowing coals, and partially burnt remnants of whatever had been inside. His tent still stood, but not for much longer. The flames gobbled the oiled cloth and licked at the wooden poles. Trunks and tables had been dragged outside, well away from the fire. As had much of his extra armor and weaponry. He caught hold of a man bent beneath a pole laden with overflowing buckets. "Where is she? Or Hendry? Where is he?"

The warrior, known only as Banyan, backed up a step. His eyes flared wide in his smoke-blackened face. "I dinna ken, m'lord. Only been toting water and dirt to save what I could. Them arrows of theirs be soaked in a pitch that willna die easy."

"On wi' ye then." He wouldn't hold the man up. He'd search for Adellis himself. With a mighty yank, he pulled a burning arrow out of Hendry's spice trunk and tried stamping out the flames. Banyan spoke the truth. Whatever pitch or oil they coated the arrows with only splattered and spread. With enough dirt piled on it, he finally smothered the fire.

"Adellis!" With long strides around the periphery of the camp, he searched and bellowed her name over and over. No clues or signs existed that gave him any hope she might be alive and hidden somewhere among them. He found little comfort in the fact that he had not come across her lifeless body.

A wider pass around the area took him into the woods next to his burning tent. His heart lurched at the sight of a hand, limp and pale, reaching out from the base of a tree, its owner hidden on the other side. He crashed through the thicket, then blew out a relieved burst of air. It was Edrid. He had died. Just as Adellis feared he would. A look back at the remains of his tent didn't reveal how the spy's body had come to be among the trees.

"M'lord." A rasping whisper that sounded more like the croaking of a frog made him turn.

"Hendry!"

The lad stumbled forward.

He caught him and gently lowered him to his knees. The usually spotless linen of the knave's tunic was torn, bloody, and blackened with soot. "Where ye be hurt, lad? How bad?"

The boy shook his head and patted shaking fingers toward his shoulder. "Arrow got me there, but it isna bad at all." Then tears welled in his deep brown eyes. He turned his face away with an embarrassed jerk. "I failed ye, m'lord. Pray forgive me. I beg ye."

Thorburn's heart sank lower. He knew without asking what Hendry spoke of. "Did ye see them take her?"

"Nay." The boy jerked his head from side to side. His tangled mat of ruddy hair fell across his face. "They was so quiet. When I ran to the place where I heard her last, all I seen was splatters of blood and tracks dug deep from the struggle. She didna go easy. I dinna ken what they did to her or even if she still lives. All I know for certain is that it looked like more than one took her." His face twisted with the horror of reliving the moment. "Then the burning arrows came. From everywhere. Like God sending fire down from the heavens." He hitched in a shuddering breath, face crumpling as his tears flowed faster. "Forgive me for failing ye, m'lord. I am so ashamed."

"Ye have brought no shame upon yerself, Hendry." Thorburn examined the wound in the lad's shoulder. The burning pitch from the arrow had cauterized the puncture and trapped the blood. A purple knot swelled beneath his pale skin. It needed lancing and flushing out before cauterizing it again to heal proper. Hendry had always acted the healer if a true one couldn't be found. The task would fall to either Ross or Valan's provision knaves, Munro or Marcas. "How much time has passed since they took her?"

Hendry wiped his face on his sleeve, then stared out into space, his eyes narrowing to slits as he pondered. "They struck not long after ye rode out." He frowned and made a face. "Mayhap close to an hour after the last of the guard disappeared beyond the hill. Yer lady and I got Edrid to the shade and sorted through all that we needed to tend him proper." He shook his head. "That's why she went into the woods. To gather more resin to mix with the myrrh." He cast a sorrowful gaze downward. "She wanted him fit to send back to his family on the next ship." He lifted his head. "For one from the north, she didna seem so hate-filled and cold as I'd always heard."

That observation made Thorburn smile. He stood and helped Hendry to his feet. "It doesna matter where a person is from. That isna what makes them bad or good. It's their heart that does that. Not where they're born. My mother was from Norway."

"Beg pardon, m'lord." The knave ducked his head again. "Meant no disrespect."

"I must see to the others now." Thorburn helped the boy limp over to the trunks that had been saved from the fires. "Rest yerself 'til the guard returns. They should arrive soon, then Marcus or Munro can help ye."

"I canna rest." The servant shook his head and busied himself with sorting through the rubble, searching for more to salvage. "When they return, will ye set out to fetch her tonight?"

He wanted to set out now, but common sense and past battles held him in check. "I must think first. Gather more information." The fact they had lost Edrid, their best scout, their finder of secrets, dealt an immeasurable blow to preparing a counterattack. He would do whatever it took to recover Adellis, but he would nay walk into it blind. Scanning his men and their knaves as they toiled to recover from the carnage, he pondered who might be the best to take Edrid's place.

"Wylie," Hendry said as he lifted the lid to one of the smaller trunks and peered inside. "All my candles are a feckin' mess, m'lord."

"What?"

"A feckin' mess," the knave repeated, slamming the lid shut. "I'll have to chop them apart and make do until we return to Duart and better can be found."

Thorburn scrubbed a hand across his mouth to keep from snapping at the lad who worried more about his supplies than anything else. "What did ye mean when ye said, 'Wylie'?"

Hendry didn't look up from the contents of a trunk so large, leather strips and iron banding reinforced its scorched sides. "That Wylie be a devious wee shite. Sly as a stoat and quick as a rat. He's nay as honorable as Edrid was, but I'd bet my best cook pot he'll find out just as much. Mayhap even more." He shot a stern look over the edge of the raised lid. "I'd be happy to remind him he'll be skint alive if he doesna return with helpful things that'll aid ye in yer planning."

Hendry's uncanny ability to know what he needed before he knew it himself had always given him somewhat of an eerie feeling. But it saved time, and Hendry served him better than any knave he had ever known. For that, especially now, Thorburn was more than a little grateful. "Fetch him. The sooner I send him, the better."

The dedicated lad managed a smile for the first time since Thorburn had arrived back at what was left of the camp. With a pudgy hand pressed to his sore shoulder, he limped away in search of the new spy.

As Thorburn looked around the decimated camp, he soothed himself with the knowledge that soon, very soon, he would bring down the fires of hell upon those who dared steal away the woman he had decided to claim for his own.

ADELLIS ASSESSED HER surroundings without moving or opening her eyes. Experience had taught that it was much safer to appear unconscious in case someone watched. Naked, sprawled belly down across a padded pallet covered in the silkiest furs, she concentrated, taking inventory of her body. A faint burning throb stung in several places across her back. Other than that, she appeared injury-free. Amazing, considering her brother's past tactics.

A sticky sweet aroma, as choking as thick smoke, lent a cloying greasiness to the air. She wanted to cough but suppressed it by sheer force of will alone. Something touched her back. Cool. Slippery. It slid across her flesh like the slimiest of eels. But she found it soothing. It eased the stinging effects of the poison Alrek had used to coat the spikes of his armor. Cowardly bastard. He had impaled her with so many of the tips, it was a wonder she still lived. She probably had the scars of her flailing to thank for her survival. The thickened skin had prevented the barbs from going too deep.

"I know my lady be awake," whispered a timid voice she didn't recognize. A young female. With a lilting accent, even more singsong than normal in the isles or Norway. A Dane perhaps? Adellis wasn't sure.

"I promise it be only us two in here, my lady," the girl continued. "I be Gerdy. Thy new slave from mighty Jarl Fridrik. I am your wedding gift."

It was all Adellis could do not to react. But she remained motionless, keeping her breathing slow and even. Jarl Fridrik? A wedding gift? Apparently, Alrek had bartered her off again. Damn him and his incessant plotting.

"I pray my lady lives longer than my previous mistresses," Gerdy continued in a hesitant whisper. "Whenever my mistresses die, I am charged with providing Jarl Fridrik with one of my fingers as punishment for failing to heal them of the wounds from his bed play." A soft sound, something akin to a shuddering sigh, accompanied a chilling sensation across the wetness of Adellis's bare shoulders. Whatever poultice covered her back had just been refreshed. "Two mistresses along with two of my fingers have been taken from me so far. I know not how many went before Jarl Fridrik's guard captured me at Akranes."

Akranes? Gerdy was from Iceland. Adellis struggled not to react. If Gerdy came from Iceland, Jarl Fridrik was none other than the odious Fridrik Gustaffson. A man known for his cruelty and penchant for torturing his wives until they died. The man collected them like trophies. She couldn't remember the last count she heard. Alrek had always admired the man and the dark rumors surrounding him. The only difference in the two was that Alrek had yet to take a wife and follow in Fridrik's footsteps.

She could tell by the brightness shining through her closed eyelids that, wherever she lay, a multitude of candles, torches, and lanterns glowed. Although Gerdy appeared to be a victim in this cruel game, too, Adellis wouldn't put it past her brother to have staged this display for all to enjoy, and the girl was but one of the players. She had witnessed such behavior in him before.

An odd whooshing of air fanned around her as though someone forced it across her. She tried not to snort at the sickening fragrance hitting her full in the face. For an aroma to be so stout, they couldn't be in the large, tented amphitheater Alrek ordered erected upon their arrival on Mull. Unlike the *Gallóglaigh*, her brother delighted in taking prisoners for cruel entertainment. Nay. They had to be in a much smaller enclosure, and Gerdy's heavy use of the incense made the air of the place chewable.

"I swear I will help my lady escape if you take me as well or end my suffering with a blade. I beg you, my lady."

Unable to harness her curiosity any longer, Adellis risked cracking open an eyelid. From what little she could see, they were in a small enclosure, perhaps one of the compact tent lodges used for steam bathing. A long, shallow ceramic bowl rested on a short-legged table beside the low platform on which she lay. It was filled with wide strips of some kind of dark green substance that floated in a congealed-looking liquid. A pair of small hands came into view, selected one of the strips, and smoothed the stickiness off it. A clear ooze slithered down the length of the greenness and glopped back into the bowl. Then renewed wetness cooled her back, refreshing the numbing sensation provided by the strange poultice.

She decided the strips were some sort of leaves, then dismissed the thought. The girl's left hand held her interest. The slave hadn't lied. If Gerdy ever wished to, she wouldn't be able to wear a ring on the usual finger, nor on the smaller finger next to it. Both were missing. Adellis lifted her head and opened her eyes fully, turning to discover the wisp of a girl tending her. The pitiful slave was nothing but skin-covered bones, made to look even more frail and deathlike with a shaved head and dark soot painted around her eyes.

"How long have I been here?" Adellis asked as she pushed herself upright. The remnants of the poison still weakened her but moving would help drive the toxins away.

"It is nearly dawn of the third day." Gerdy scrambled up on the platform beside her and gently peeled the muck off her back. She dabbed away the remaining wetness with a soft linen.

"What is that?"

"Kelp…and other things. It draws out the poison and heals." A stark hopelessness filled the girl's tone, making her speech almost painful to hear.

Adellis turned and caught hold of Gerdy's wrist. "If you let them take away your hope and your spirit, they will defeat you."

"Then I am defeated, my lady."

"It cannot be." Adellis gave her an encouraging nod. "You bargained to help me escape. That speaks of hope and spirit that remains."

Gerdy's mouth twitched as though trying to remember how to smile. "How? Where would we go?"

"Anywhere is better than here. Would you not agree?"

"Yes." The girl rose, went to a door flap Adellis hadn't noticed, and listened. Even in her emaciated state, she appeared brighter. "No one stirs yet." She pointed at the bowl of kelp, then at the smoking brazier in the corner. "Once your body purges all of Jarl Alrek's poison, I have orders to tell the guards you are ready for sentencing and the ceremony."

"What has the pompous fool planned for me this time?" Adellis managed to stand, stretching and demanding her muscles to awaken and come alive.

"You are to be given the choice of marriage to Jarl Fridrik or death by nailing to the Tree of Woe."

"The Tree of Woe is on Normandy's shores." Had Alrek's madness robbed him of his sense of direction?

"I heard Jarl Alrek boast that any tree on this Isle could be made into the Tree of Woe." Gerdy scurried back from the doorway and rubbed down Adellis's back, legs, and arms until a vibrancy tingled across her flesh. Tossing the cloth aside, she scooped out a handful of a thick white paste from a small crock and massaged it in until it disappeared, leaving behind a healthy glow. "He has even offered to allow his archers to make sport by using you as a target."

"How generous of him."

Gerdy's sooty eyes rounded even wider. "You do not fear

him?"

"My hunger for revenge has driven out any fear I once had. I refuse to be Alrek's amusement ever again." She stumbled to the tent flap, fighting against the heaviness plaguing her limbs. Peering at the night, she made out nothing at first. Only an eerie darkness, layers of shadows, some darker, some lighter, but all an otherworldly black. Only the occasional flickering of a torch could be seen floating through the fog beyond the enclosure. "It is too quiet. Neither he nor his slaves ever sleep. Where is he?"

"Gone to finish those who took you. Then on to the castle to raze it to the ground for the last time." Gerdy wiped her hands on the rough cloth she wore swaddled around her body like a wrap for the dead. "It is said he saves you for last. As part of his victory celebration. Jarl Fridrik's guard is due to arrive within days to fetch you. Then you will be required to make your choice."

"Gone to finish those who took me," Adellis repeated, disregarding everything else the girl had said. Thorburn. Her Scottish bear. Alrek would not fight him with honor. He hunted down those he hated. Preyed upon them. She feared Thor, her mighty warrior, would not be prepared for the sort of devilry her brother possessed. Her Scottish bear would fall.

"Does your breast pain you, my lady?"

"What?" Adellis stared at the girl. "Why would you ask such a question?"

Gerdy hesitantly touched the fist Adellis unconsciously clutched to her chest. "Do you hurt inside? Your heart or where you breathe? I have brews that could help. Smoke you could breathe."

"A brew will not help." Adellis let her hand fall away and turned back to peering outside. She had been stricken with the strongest poison of all. A dangerous caring. Such a fool she was. She knew better. How in God's name had that stubborn Scot foisted such a feeling upon her?

Escape was even more important now. She had to find him. Warn him. He had to be kept safe. Even if she had to break her oath and kill her brother. Mother's spirit would somehow forgive her. "How many remain here? You mentioned you were to report to the guards?"

Gerdy joined her at the opening, pointed to the east, and then to the west. "Naught but two remain. Wherever you see torch light. Jarl Alrek felt sure his poison would keep you close to death until he returned." A proud smile finally curved the girl's mouth, adding a much-needed roundness to her hollow cheeks. "He did not know of my kelp poultice's power."

The knowledge that Alrek's conceit had played against him once again filled Adellis with thankfulness. Many times, his overconfidence had been his worst enemy and her greatest weapon. "Good then. We must move fast." She took notice of every article cluttering the small den. "I need clothing and your sharpest blades." She peered outside again, craning her neck to squint up at the starless sky. Perfect. The dark of the moon and a cloudy night. Both would serve her well. She turned back and eyed Gerdy. "You need garb that will let you run, crouch, or climb. Shed those rags. Drink and eat while I dress. You do not appear strong at all."

"I am stronger than I look."

"You will need to be." Adellis rolled her shoulders, impressed that nothing bothered her but a faint soreness. Gerdy's healing skills seemed close to miraculous. She joined the girl at a pair of open trunks on one end of the pallet. The trunk to the right had an assortment of folded clothing piled inside. The other held an array of tools, bundles, and bottles that she assumed were used for healing. A dagger-like instrument, long, thin, and with a slight curve to the blade made her smile. "I want that one."

Gerdy pulled it free of the leather loop holding it in place and offered it, along with a stack of dark clothing from the other trunk. "There is no food here. Nor drink."

The girl looked ready to faint. If she didn't eat, Adellis had her doubts she would make it. She tipped her head toward the doorway. "Tell them you need food to tempt me back to consciousness. Tell them your healing is helping, but you fear it is not enough to pull me through."

After a hesitant step toward the exit, Gerdy paused and turned back. "But they will bring it in here. They do not allow me near their stores. They fear I will poison them."

"Not a bad idea." Adellis mulled it over but decided against it. It wasn't worth the effort or loss of time to poison just two guards. She would finish the men off with a blade. "Let them come. I will be ready." Another tool, one that consisted of a long, wicked spike protruding from a chunk of carved antler, caught her eye. "I will have that one, too. Once I've sent the guards to the other side, I'll take their swords and daggers, and you can use these if need be."

Gerdy's face paled even more, making the soot around her eyes more fearsome. The sight gave Adellis another idea. "If we soot our faces completely, we will be harder to see in case we come across any guards Alrek has left along the way."

"Why would he do that?" The tiny healer frowned as she touched a hand to her face.

"Because that is what he does." She rested a hand on the girl's bony shoulder. "We will prevail if we refuse to fear defeat."

"But we could be defeated," Gerdy whispered.

"How bad do you want your freedom and a new life?" Adellis stood taller, fixing the waif with a fierce smile. Doubt could be a warrior's worst enemy. It must not be allowed.

"More than anything."

"Then fight for it and do not consider defeat."

Gerdy pulled in a deep breath, blew it out, then lifted her chin. "To freedom."

Adellis smiled and squeezed the girl's shoulder. "To freedom." *And saving my Scottish bear*, she added silently.

CHAPTER SEVEN

THORBURN SCOWLED DOWN at the encampment on the beach below. It was too still. Too calm. What if they were too late?

The blackness of the night allowed little to be seen other than a pair of torches bobbing past a faint flickering of light escaping from underneath the walls of at least two shelters. From the outline of the glow, one was a tent that was quite small, and another appeared large enough for a legion of men. Waves crashed across the rocky shoreline bordering the place. A nearby waterfall tumbled down a steep cliffside. The night revealed no other sounds of what should have been a noisy outpost of rogue Northmen.

"I canna believe Edrid failed to find this place," Thorburn muttered, speaking more to himself than his brothers.

"He didna search this far west. Just moved northward along the Sound." Ross shifted positions and made a sweeping motion that took in the camp. "They chose a good place. Near as I can tell, there is only one way to reach them." He pointed at a less treacherous spot farther down the shore.

"Keep yer voice down, man," Valan scolded. "We dinna ken if there be more guards up here, and our men are still position-ing."

The *Gallóglaigh* had as fine a set of archers as the men from the north. Thorburn had ordered them to find good vantage points whilst the rest of the men readied themselves to lay siege.

His goal was rescuing Adellis.

"I see naught but two down there," he said quietly. "Mind those torches there. The way they move. Two guards for certain." They had encountered and killed six so far, and none of the curs had seen fit to tell them anything that might aid them in their cause. It appeared Alrek's men feared his wrath more than they feared death. "This darkness might conceal us, but it hides them, too."

A large square of light flashed from the smallest tent, but once the flap fell back in place, the velvety darkness blotted out everything once again. The two torches, separated by several lengths, converged as though their bearers now stood together. Thorburn snorted out a frustrated huff. They needed to get closer. If there was naught but the two, they could dispatch them easily and save the rest of the men for battle when they came across the entirety of Alrek's forces.

He knew that he and his brothers could find and recover Adellis before the Northmen realized their enclosure had been breached. Just to be certain, the entire fourscore and ten of his *Gallóglaigh* waited for the signal to attack. He would spare nothing when it came to recovering his fierce vixen from the north.

He stood and gave Tasgall the signal to notify the men to stand ready to charge. Time was at hand. "Enough waiting."

Ross and Valan stayed close on his heels as they picked their way down the grassy hillside riddled with stones that threatened to roll with every step. The cloudy night and blanket of mist settling in the low spots cursed them as well as benefited them. An occasional dip in the land and the few mounds of boulders did little to hide them.

Thorburn picked up speed as the ground evened out. Focused on the torches still fairly close together, he moved with the silent stealth taught by his father while training at his side. When they drew close enough to make out the dark shapes of more tents, he halted. Every muscle knotted tighter. Alrek's numbers appeared to be a great deal more than first reported. A single monstrosity of a structure sprawled across the beachhead. Several smaller shelters extended out from either side like a great bird's outstretched wings. Had Alrek coerced half of Norway to fight at his side?

He took cover behind one of the smaller tents, eased to the edge, then peered around. Nothing but shadows and swirling mist. The torches had disappeared. Rather than growling out his frustration, he clenched his teeth and snorted. Which shelter had the fools entered? He strained to hear something other than the incessant crashing of the sea. Nothing came to him. There was naught to do but move forward and search.

With a signal to his brothers, he eased around the shelter with his sword and dagger leading the way. Patience exhausted and senses alerted to the slightest movement or sound, he headed to the largest structure first. The place was probably the gathering area for food and drink. Since both torches disappeared, it was likely the men had gone in there.

With the tip of his sword, he eased open the flap and peered inside. A pair of great iron torch stands burned brightly on either side of a garishly opulent chair, overflowing with cushions. What a sight. Adellis's brother must think himself either a king or a god. Benches and tables lined the sides of the massive tent. The center area remained bare, as though waiting for entertainment. He let the flap fall back in place and shook his head at Ross, who, in turn, shook his head at Valan.

That left the other tent that had shown light within it. He resettled his grip on his weapons. The leather-wrapped hafts scraped rough against his palms, adding fuel to his fiery hunger for victory and revenge. As he started toward the shelter, light flashed from the opening and halted him. Two cloaked figures, one quite a bit taller than the other, stood silhouetted in the doorway as though gathering their bearings. He strained to make out what was behind them. Two bodies appeared to be sprawled on the ground inside. Against all instinct and training, he called out in a loud whisper, "Adellis!"

The tallest of the two turned toward him. "Thor?"

"Adellis," he repeated, breathing out her name to soothe his soul. He tore forward and crushed her to his chest. "Thank God," he whispered, reveling in the feel of her. He buried his face in the rough fabric of her cloak.

She flinched and squeaked out a cry of pain that cut through him like a dagger. With a jagged gasp, she pushed against him. "Easy, my bear. Gerdy healed me, but there is still some soreness across my back."

He immediately eased his hold, cradling her in one arm as he shoved back her hood. "What did that bastard do to…" Her soot-covered face, now streaked with two shining paths cleared away by tears, struck him speechless.

"To better hide us in the darkness," she explained with such a caring touch of his cheek that his heart soared.

"Ye can celebrate yer reunion once we're clear of here," Ross advised, shoving around them to nudge a boot against a man on the floor. He looked up and grinned. "Yer lady did well, brother."

"Come," Valan urged. "Ross is right. We can raise a glass once we clear the place. Our men dinna wait well, ye ken?"

Thorburn agreed. Adellis could tell him all that had happened once they withdrew. "Are there more here to be dealt with?"

She turned to her companion, the tiny figure, cowering so deep in a dark, ragged cloak that her face couldn't be seen. "Gerdy, these two are all. Yes?"

Gerdy didn't speak, just dipped her hooded head forward.

"We owe them one more thing before we leave." The need for revenge ran deep in every fiber of his being. Always had. It made him the commander he was today. "We shall signal the men that all is well with a fine fire, ye ken?" He gave his brothers a knowing look they couldn't help but understand.

Ross yanked a torch from its stand and held it against the wall of the tent until the flames caught hold. Valan grinned and headed outside to do the same to the other shelters.

"The boats as well," Adellis suggested. "Pitch and arrows are in the tent farthest to the east. The longboats are anchored offshore in front of the waterfall and the cave. If we send fiery brands across the water, we should be able to see them well enough to set them ablaze."

He caught hold of her hand, pressed a kiss into her palm, then eased her closer. All that he witnessed in her clear blue eyes made his chest tighten. Relief. Joy. And what he hoped was the same urgent need that pounded through him, all because of her. Not just a longing for a touch or a joining, but a dangerous yearning he had never experienced before.

"Ye are mine," he rasped, then sealed the declaration with the kiss he had hungered for ever since the taste of the last one had faded. All else could be damned. Her warmth spread through him. The hardness of her warrior's form and the softness of her curves melted into his embrace. With her fingers tangled deep in his hair, she dug in her nails as she claimed him with as much fervor as he claimed her. Never again. Nothing would separate them ever again.

"My lady, the tent burns around you." The soft, squeaking voice barely wormed its way between them. "My lady—please."

The wee one was right. Regret filled him as he gently severed their connection and smiled down at her. "Are ye sound enough to stay at my side whilst we make quick work of yer brother's holdings?"

"Yes, my fine warrior. Consider yourself most definitely burdened with me now." The smile she gave him erased any weariness he had ever known.

"For that, I am grateful." He ushered both her and the small cloaked one out of the flames' reach and headed to the tent containing the tools that would aid them in burning all signs of Alrek away. Ross and Valan joined them, both looking well pleased with themselves. When the hollow roaring of a well-fed fire reached him, Thorburn understood why. The only tent not ablaze was the one in front of them.

Inside, he helped himself to the weaponry that had probably been used to destroy his own camp and wound poor Hendry. He would take great pleasure in setting the long boats afire. 'Twas a shame Hendry had stayed with the men and couldn't help. Such a loss would be costly to any campaign, but especially to one as covert as Alrek's.

Adellis pushed in beside him, snatching a longbow out of his grasp. "This one is mine," she said with a tip of her head toward another. "You can have that one."

"As ye wish, m'love."

She paused, her brow furrowing for a split second as though the endearment had struck her like a dart.

He smiled. She heard it as he had meant it this time. "Aye, m'love." With a slow shaking of his head, he picked up the bow she had pointed out. "It is no longer friendship I seek."

She didn't speak, but her faint smile, barely discernible through the grime of her sooty face, reassured him that perhaps she no longer looked for anything as mild as friendship either.

As soon as they removed all the pitch and weapons needed, the roaring blaze from the adjacent tent took over and engulfed that last one as well. It was as though the gods held the flames at bay until they recovered everything they needed. The timing wasn't lost on Thorburn. Superstition ran as swift and sure in his veins as blood.

"Come," he said, waving them onward toward the falls. "It is past time to end this."

Adellis took the first shot, lighting a path out over the water that revealed the shadowy outline of three longboats floating side by side.

He timed his close behind, a flood of satisfaction filling him as the blazing bolt found its mark and set to gnawing into the vessel nestled between the other two.

Adellis fired again, spearing the ship to the right.

Ross and Valan shot in tandem, their brands setting fire to the third.

"We have done well here," Thorburn observed. "That should redden his arse for him."

"If he bothers to return," Adellis commented. The fires lit her worried frown. With her bow clutched to her side, she gave his forearm an urgent squeeze. "He marches on Duart. Intends to raze it to the ground and kill all that claim fealty to the Lord of Argyll, King Magnus, or your Alexander of Scotland." She settled a precious touch to his cheek. "I sought to warn you. Gerdy helped with my healing and escape. I beg you grant her your protection as well."

He covered her hand with his and smiled. "Ye need not beg for anything, m'lady. Whatever ye wish is yers."

Gerdy shoved back her hood, revealing her shaved head and otherworldly appearance. "It is true, my lord. Please have no doubt of my lady's word." She clutched her hands to her chest, fell to her knees, and bowed her head.

"I do not doubt her," he hurried to reassure the strange girl. "Rise, lass. Ye have nothing to fear." What torture had Alrek foisted upon this waif?

"When did he leave for Duart?" Thorburn had left a small legion of their original landing party standing guard at the castle but didn't wish them to be the ones to enjoy taking Alrek's head. That pleasure belonged to him alone. Or, perhaps, to Adellis. If she needed such closure to heal, he would not deny her that right.

"A day ago," Gerdy whispered without looking up.

"On foot or mounts?" Thorburn scrubbed a hand across his face. A day ahead of them. They would be hard-pressed to overtake them before they reached the eastern shore.

"Alrek never rides." Adellis wet the tail of her cloak in the freshwater tumbling down the cliffside and wiped the soot from her face. "He fears all animals because they hate him."

"Animals can smell evil."

"And he does not travel nor attack at night," she added with a smug look as she shed the cloak and handed it to Gerdy. "Nor when it storms or merely rains. He believes the spirit world too close at those times."

"How the hell does he overcome anyone?" Ross asked, then shook his head. "That's feckin' pitiful."

"Beneficial," Thorburn corrected. "How many are in his ranks?"

With a pinched look, Adellis shook her head. "That I do not know. Especially since he has recruited so many from the villages."

He turned to Gerdy. "Do ye ken, lass?"

She cowered and shook her head, lifting an arm as though she feared he would strike her. "Many, my lord. I am sorry. The number, I do not know."

Her behavior pained him. With any hope, time would teach her that he did not beat women or children. Thorburn held out a hand to Adellis. "Do ye feel whole enough to ride? We should make haste."

She stared at him, her hands slowly curling into fists as she clutched them to her middle.

"Adellis?"

"I have never ridden." She avoided his gaze with an embarrassed tucking of her chin.

Thorburn smiled. He had never thought to find anything that made this fine woman hesitate.

"Do not smile at me like that." All embarrassment disappeared, and her usual stern fearlessness settled firmly back in place.

He pulled her into his arms. "Ye will ride with me. We nay have any extra horses."

She nipped his chin with her teeth, then kissed it. "You are forgiven, then."

"The little one can ride with me," Valan offered.

"Thank you, my lord," Gerdy whispered, then gave him a proper curtsy. She turned to Adellis. "With your permission, my lady?"

"Of course, Gerdy." Adellis rested a hand on the girl's shoulder. "Courage and hope. Remember?"

The frail lass brightened, dipped another curtsy, then obediently fell in step behind Valan and Ross.

"Has she told ye the horrors she has been through?" Thorburn asked as they left the cinder- and ash-filled shore and headed to where his men stood fast until given the signal to charge.

"Some." Adellis stared downward, holding tight to his arm as she picked her way across the rough terrain.

He noticed her labored breathing and struggling to keep pace. Without a word, he swept her up into his arms, cradling her like a babe. Before she could argue, he cut her off, "*Haud yer wheesht,* woman. Haste is a must, and it isna that far to the horses."

When she didn't argue and instead rested her head on his shoulder, he knew her to be more weakened from her ordeal than she admitted.

"Besides," he continued. "I need ye back in my arms. Dinna deny me this simple pleasure, aye?"

"I missed you, too, my Scottish bear." Her quiet tone echoed with relief. The contentment in her sigh warmed his heart, giving him the strength to carry her to the ends of the earth if need be. She brushed a tender kiss to his neck. "Are you certain we can reach Duart before Alrek?"

"If we knew whether he took the route to the north or to the south around Ben More and Dùn da Ghaoithe, it would help." Southward of both mountains was the swifter path to the east side of the isle, but would Alrek know that?

"Always before, we went to the north."

"Why?" That made no sense at all. Even one who didn't know Mull would veer southward because of the terrain.

She tensed, then shifted in his arms. "Because Alrek is a fool. He always goes to the north. Says it brings him good fortune and blessings from the gods because of our blood." She straightened and pressed her forehead to his cheek. "How much farther, my bear? Surely, my weight grows heavy for you."

"Ye insult me, m'lady." And he meant it. How dare she think

him weak. He wasn't even out of breath. "Just beyond yon ridge await the men and horses."

"I meant no insult," she said, her voice strained. "If you must know, the pressure of your arm against my back pains me."

Guilt flooded him. How could he be so thoughtless? Especially when she had mentioned her injuries earlier. With the greatest ease, he set her to her feet. "Forgive me, m'love. I am a selfish brute who thought of nothing other than the pleasure of holding ye."

"There is nothing to forgive." She leaned into him and patted both hands on his chest. "Were you bare rather than covered in mail, I would enjoy your embrace a great deal more." With a suggestive smile, she tickled her fingertips through the stubble of his beard, sending a shiver down his spine. "We have much pleasuring to enjoy once we have bested Alrek."

Avoiding her wounded back, he cupped the firm, full round-ness of her bottom in both hands and pulled her closer. "That we do, m'love. That we do." It was all he could do to force himself to release her, but they had yet to cross the ridge and descend into the glen below. With a reluctant groan, he set her an arm's length away, turned his back to her, and dropped to one knee. "Yer ride, m'lady."

"What?"

He glanced back over his shoulder. "Get on, ye ken? Straddle my back. I can hold yer legs whilst ye wrap yer arms around my neck and hold on. 'Twill make the last of the way to the glen easier on ye. Surely, ye did this when ye were a wee bairn?"

She stood there, staring down at him. Arms folded. Head tilted to one side. "You jest."

He gave her a teasing wink. "Are ye scairt?"

"I am not." Her offended tone rang loud and clear.

He faced forward again, knowing the dare would goad her into doing it. Arms akimbo, he waited. "If ye're nay too scairt, then come, m'lady. We must be on our way."

After snorting like a bull about to charge, she clambered

aboard and wrapped a choke hold around his neck.

He allowed himself a smile and patted the arm she held under his chin. "Now, now, dinna be cross. Loosen up a wee bit, or yer fine stallion canna breathe." He hooked his arms behind her knees and stood. He patted her tunic-covered rump before taking off at a brisk pace. "Now then, is this nay easier on yer back?"

"On my back? Yes. But your chain mail threatens to gnaw into my legs—among other things." She hitched herself higher, clamping her bare legs tighter around his sides.

"Dinna fash yerself, dear one, I swear to kiss away all the hurts." He bit his lip, wishing he hadn't reminded himself of the velvety softness of her inner thighs and the perfect slipperiness between. God's beard, if he kept this up, he'd not be able to walk for his tent-pole of a cock. "Just a wee bit farther," he whispered to himself. He smiled as a horse's snort echoed up ahead.

"What?" She wormed her way higher, nearly crouching atop his shoulders.

That possibility made him harder still. He had to get his mind off her bare arse and the other tempting niceties exposed every time the tail of her oversized léine flapped in the wind. "I asked what happened to the fine leather trews Hendry found for ye?"

"I have no idea." She hugged her cheek against his head and adjusted again, looping one long, lovely leg over his shoulder while the other wrapped around his front. "This is worse than enduring your touch across the wounds on my back. Pray, let me down. I will walk."

"Ye have no boots either, m'love."

"I am well aware of all that I do not have." Lifting her chin as he lowered her to her feet, she forced a smile that he barely saw in the darkness. "What I choose to dwell upon is all that I do have."

"And what is that, m'love?"

"I have my freedom." She paused long enough to stir doubt within him. "And I have my Scottish bear."

"Yer Scottish bear wishes for another kiss from his lady love," he said as he took care to pull her into his arms without touching her back.

"Your lady love," she repeated, looking up at him as though she couldn't believe her eyes. "A *Gallóglaigh* who believes in love?"

"Aye," he whispered. "Ye have conquered me, my fearless woman of the north."

"We have much to do before we do this." The strain in her tone revealed she needed him as much as he needed her. "Use this fire in battle, mighty Thor." She drew back, and even in the cloaking darkness, he saw the glint in her eyes. "I promise you will be well rewarded."

"I shall hold ye to that." He offered his arm to her.

She took it. "Somehow, you do not make me feel weak or…less when you do such things."

"I would never purposely do such." He was not a man of words, but the need to say more tightened like a band of iron around his chest. "I admire you, Adellis, and…"

"And?"

"And I care."

She made an amused sound, a lilting hum, as if she laughed with her mouth tightly closed.

"Ye think my words foolish?"

"No. I think you are the first man who has ever cared whether I lived or died and…"

The way she paused made him hunger to hear the rest of her thought. "And?"

"And I like that. Very much."

CHAPTER EIGHT

ADELLIS WIGGLED HER toes in the makeshift boots Hendry had fashioned from a spare weapons tote Tasgall had donated. The pliable leather felt odd lashed around her feet and calves, but he had doubled the material across the soles so rough terrain no longer pained her. She was grateful for the knave's talent at creating something out of nothing. Fighting barefoot always resulted in wounded feet.

Someone had found her a pair of trews as well. She smiled at that. Thorburn hadn't wished her to be a distraction to his men. Or so he said. His possessive squeeze of her bottom as he gave the order revealed his jealousy. A treat she had never known before. It felt both strange and wonderful.

A belt with loops held bolts and arrows for the bow she had procured from Alrek's tent. A dagger, long enough to be considered a small sword, had also been found. Most of the men considered that weapon too womanish, preferring their heavy spears, axes, and massive two-handed swords. She didn't care that her blade seemed small to them. When she slit her brother's throat, she preferred to be close enough for a good look into his eyes. She wanted Alrek to know without a doubt who had killed him.

A subtle shifting in the saddle did little in finding a more comfortable position without Thorburn noticing. While she agreed that traveling by horse would get them to the castle ahead of Alrek, she had yet to decide if she enjoyed riding. Perhaps, it would nay be so trying if she still wasn't expelling the remains of Alrek's poison at every half mark of the hour.

"Do ye need to stop again, lass?"

"I fear so." She huffed out her shame. Never had she pissed so much in all her life. Gerdy assured her it was because of the kelp poultice and brew she kept making her drink. The girl also told her she should be glad of it. All Adellis knew was they didn't have time for all these incessant stops. "Forgive me," she said as he lowered her to the ground.

"Gerdy said it is a good thing. Helps ye heal. Therefore, it must be so." His understanding smile made her feel even worse.

She squatted behind a large rock and let loose enough water to create a small fjord. As she balanced against the stone and continued the steady stream, a flash of light from the faded blue-gray rise of land north of them caught her attention. "Thorburn!"

"Aye?" He stepped into view, revealing he had dismounted and stood guard to ensure her privacy.

"There." She pointed as she yanked up her trews and straightened her clothes. "I saw the sun bounce off steel. Right where the second hill dips down and joins the third. Watch that line of shadows at the base of the ridge. How it shifts. That is the darkness of an army moving."

Eyes narrowed, he focused on the area.

She stared at the spot as well, every muscle tightening as the movement of Alrek's numbers became easier to make out. The cunning fool had shifted tactics, taken to the south rather than the north. She turned to apologize for giving such poor advice regarding her vile sibling, but instead, found herself struck silent.

Thorburn's strong, fierce stance sent a tingle through her like the strike of nearby lightning. His light hair gleamed in the sunlight, and the stubble of his short beard glinted like gold. He shone like a godlike warrior of light, made even more breathtaking when he took to his saddle on a stallion blacker than the darkest night.

He reached down for her. "Come, I feel sure they have seen us."

She paused a moment, scanning the area, assessing its advantages and shortcomings. This would not be a terrible place to battle—if they could convince Alrek to turn and engage rather than charge on to Duart. She took his hand and launched herself back into place in front of him. "We should bait him to fight us here. Would that not be better than risking those working on the castle?"

Thorburn hugged an arm around her middle but didn't pull her back against his chest. His continued mindfulness of her tender back stirred a dangerous softness in her heart, a softness she needed to harden and set aside whilst they battled. Warring called for concentration. Especially when her Scot and all he cared about were at risk.

He turned the horse. "I prefer we meet at Duart. We should easily beat them there and join with the rest of our number."

While she didn't necessarily agree, she yielded without argument. This had become more than a battle between herself and her brother. This had become a scourging to ensure that not only Alrek fell, but that no others dared take up their swords and continue his cause.

Thorburn spurred his mount into a full gallop. His men followed suit. Fifty *Gallóglaigh* shook the earth, charging across the land. They streamed out onto the peninsula to the nearly completed fortress. Perched atop a rocky crag, the stone fortification looked out upon the channel, not only controlling it but also Lochs Linne and Etive and the neck of the Firth of Lorne where the waterways joined the Sound of Mull. Duart Castle. A powerful holding. Her Scottish bear had been correct. This was the perfect place for Alrek to fall.

Adellis sat taller, impressed by the legion of men standing guard atop the completed portions of the walls and on either side of the steps leading to the narrow, arched entry. As Thorburn helped her dismount, she admired the work of the stonemasons.

To carve and fit such an array of different shaped stones, and all while under attack, took dedicated artisans, indeed.

"They should reach us soon." Thorburn signaled his brothers, the lines around his mouth tightening as he looked out upon what would soon be a battlefield. His gaze slid to her. "I ken well enough the foolishness of the request I am about to make—"

She cut him off with a look and a hand pressed to his chest. "I must face him. For all that has happened between us, I must do this. I will not run from him any longer. This is not just a matter of my freedom anymore. It is many wrongs that need to be made right."

He took hold of her shoulders and pulled her close, staring into her eyes with a raging intensity that shouted his unspoken fears. "I need ye safe. Whole," he rasped. "I willna bear losing ye again."

"My soul will not rest until I settle this." She knew of no way to make him understand. The realization had taken forever to make itself known to her. This lifelong battle with her twin must end. Today. "I will be fine, my ferocious bear." The high wall gave her a compromise to offer him some small ease. "I will take to the wall, yes? Use my bow for as long as possible and steer clear of the fray."

Relief flickered in the storming blue of his eyes. "Aye," he agreed after a long pause filled with so much frustration the air crackled.

Ross and Valan appeared. Their knaves, loaded down with a wide assortment of extra weapons, followed close on their heels. Thorburn's attendants had yet to show with his additional spears, axes, and blades.

"Where are Hendry and Tasgall? They should be at your side by now." Adellis craned her neck, searching for the young men entrusted to serve her mighty bear.

"They search for armor and more weapons for yerself." Thorburn shielded his eyes, watching the neck of the peninsula for Alrek's arrival.

Adellis smiled. Not because of what he had said, but because of his concentration. It comforted her. Such focus would keep him alive. She pulled on his arm. "A kiss, my love, before I go to the wall."

His focus whipped away from the approaching army and locked on her. *"M'love?"* His hand slid along her jaw and tipped back her head. "Ye usually address me as yer *bear*, m'lady."

She caressed his cheek, his short beard tickling her palm. "You will always be my *Scottish bear*, but you are now also *my love*." She breathed him in, forever storing his scent in every fiber. With a teasing smile, she angled her chin to an imperious slant. "You should be honored. I do not bestow the title lightly."

"I am, m'love," he whispered, then took her mouth with his.

She clung to him for as long as she dared, then forced herself to tear free and run up the stairs without looking back. The possessiveness of his kiss gave her strength, sent her into battle with the confidence she needed. She strode to the highest point, climbing to where no other dared to perch.

"M'lady!"

Balanced on the narrow path running atop the curtain wall stood Tasgall and Hendry. Tasgall held up a cumbersome hauberk of chain mail, a dented helmet, and a shield. Hendry wrestled with a spiked mace, an oversized axe, and a spear. "Please come down, so's I can help ye ready yerself," Tasgall called out. "M'lord has so ordered it."

Never would she keep her balance if she donned all that garb and attempted a return to her pinnacle. "Leave it there and go to your master. Protect him. That is your duty."

Both scowled up at her as if trying to figure out how to knock her from her perch. "But m'lord wishes ye fully armored, m'lady," Hendry said, squinting one eye shut against the glare of the sun. He pointed at the weapons propped against the battlement. "And ye will need these, too."

"I will come down once my bolts are spent." A glance told her that her kin would soon be upon them. "Hie to your master.

Keep him provided with the weaponry he needs. Now!" She knocked an arrow. "Or I will shoot you."

They stared up at her with their hands fisted, looking like a pair of sullen children. "M'lord will not be pleased with this!" Tasgall shouted with a stomp of his foot.

"Not one bit," Hendry added as if that would sway her.

She truly didn't wish to waste any more time on these two, nor have to climb down and retrieve the arrow after she purposely missed them. With a tip of her head toward the approaching horde, she aimed at Tasgall, figuring him to be the more persuadable. "They are nearly here. Leave now, or I shoot at the count of seven. One, two, three…"

Tasgall grabbed Hendry by the shoulders and herded him back toward the stairs leading down from the parapet.

At last. She relaxed the bow and returned her attention to the Northmen charging them. It pleased her to see that the number of villagers joining Alrek's forces had dwindled. The poor folk must have finally realized that he used them for shields, always placing them at the front to meet the enemy first.

Her focus found Thorburn at the front and center of his fearsome *Gallóglaigh*, flanked by his brothers. A massive wall of muscle and fury clad in spiked helms and chain mail. Each of them was strengthened by centuries of warring passed down through their bloodline. From this vantage point, she could deter any who might attempt to breach any vulnerable spots in the fortification, as well as watch after her Scottish bear. Her brother always sent guards to creep in where least expected. She would be prepared.

As she had thought, two of the Northmen slipped over the edge of the rocky promontory providing the foundation for the castle. Their intent to clamber unseen along the cliffside was foiled by her vantage point. With patience born from years of battling to stay alive, Adellis waited for the perfect mark. A pale neck was revealed by a loosened helm on one and the upturned face of the other. Her arrows found them both and sent them tumbling into the sea.

A familiar roar shot through her, yanking her attention back to the front of the stronghold in time to see Thorburn fell three of Alrek's best. She recognized them by their breastplates, stained blood red, then marked in the center with a trio of white chevrons. If those three had made it this close, Alrek wouldn't be far behind. He kept himself surrounded by his chosen.

At last, she spied him. Even though the cowardly fool fought at the rear, he set himself out by wearing their father's helm. A red bascinet fitted with an inky black ventail and twisted horns wrought from iron. His spiked breastplate was stained red as well, lending to the effect of a demon rising from the deepest levels of Hell. While she wished to look him in the eyes when she killed him, she dared not risk him engaging Thorburn. Cowardly, Alrek might be, but also evil enough to do whatever it took to win and torture his opponent.

Adellis nocked an arrow in place and pulled back, waiting for the perfect shot. While she might be too far away to kill him, she could at least bring him to his knees. As he turned and prepared to lob a spear, she spotted her mark and released the bolt. It sank deep into his ribcage, and with any luck, made it clear to his black heart. He sagged to one knee, then fell to his side and went still. A shuddering exhale rattled out of her, and a cold sweat soaked her body.

"Forgive me, Mother," she whispered with closed eyes. When she opened them, he still hadn't moved, even when another fell across him. Even though she hated him, a jagged sense of loss sliced through her. A feeling like she had somehow killed a part of herself. She broke free of the eerie spell and scrambled down to the parapet. While skimming down the stairs to ground level, she sobbed. Jerking to a halt, she angrily swiped at the tears. What the devil was wrong with her? Why should she cry for one so vile as Alrek? Then it finally came to her. The tears were not from sorrow but release.

The ring of steel and guttural roars as warrior clashed with warrior faded to cries and groans of the wounded and the silence of the dead. She charged through the carnage, determined to look upon Alrek's face, and mayhap even spit in it.

A powerful hand pulled her about. As she thumped against his chest, she tapped the tip of her dagger against Thorburn's helm. "You should not startle me, my love, lest you find yourself piked on my blade."

He grinned before ripping off the simple bascinet and tossing it aside. "And here I thought to allay my lady love's fears as she searched in earnest for me."

She stretched to kiss him, reveling in the scent of sweat and blood while his strength encircled her. "I love the taste of a man fresh from battle." Taking care to sheath her blade, she firmly but gently pushed herself out of his arms. "But I must make sure he is dead."

"Alrek?"

"Yes."

He brushed a tender kiss across her forehead. "Lead on, m'love."

"The one in the red helm, beneath those two." She pointed as they walked around the dead and dying. A scream startled her, making her turn in time to witness one of the *Gallóglaigh* finishing off a northman with a spear.

Before she could ask, her Scottish bear explained, "I dinna take prisoners."

A chill swept across her. "You took me."

"Aye, I did." He made a long, slow scowling perusal of the bloodbath before settling a much kinder expression on her. "Ye are a woman, and I sensed a kindred spirit within ye." His face darkened like storm clouds gathering over the sea. "I willna suffer any of these men to live and take up their weapons again once we have returned to Argyll." His nostrils flared as if he smelled a stench. "I tire of this place and wish to be done with it. Do ye not feel so yerself?"

He was right to end them and hopefully prevent further

uprisings. As much as she hated to see these men die, the fact that none of them had ever attempted to help her, nor would have mourned her death, did not escape her. "Yes. I am ready to be done with Mull." She grabbed the shoulder of one of the bodies across her brother. "Help me. The red helm is who I seek."

Thorburn dragged the rest out of the way, reached for Alrek's helmet, then paused. He straightened and took a step back. "Do ye wish me to reveal him?"

"No. This is my task." She stepped forward and stared down at the closed eyes behind the ventail, eyes blackened with soot to conceal them behind the bascinet. Taking hold of the twisted iron horns of the helmet, she yanked it away, then slammed the horrendous symbol from her childhood to the ground. "It is not him," she forced through clenched teeth. "It is not Alrek."

Thorburn stared at her. His features hardened, as if a sorceress had turned him to stone. "We will find him," he swore with a low growl. "I willna rest 'til we find him."

The unknown stabbed her like a jagged blade. Mocked her. Filled her with a need to retch. "He may not have even been among them." She jerked around and stared off into the distance, wishing she had the power to envision where the sly demon hid. Another scream of a dying prisoner jolted her from her fuming. "Any who live must be questioned. Stop killing them!"

"Halt!" Thorburn's bellow cracked like thunder. All movement ceased. Even the wind stilled. "Kill no more survivors until I order it so. Find the living and call out." The order rippled from man to man, then the warriors returned to their sifting through the bodies, but slower and with more care.

"Here!" one called from beside the stone stairway leading to the arched entrance.

Adellis rushed to the dying man's side, recognizing him as one of Alrek's most loyal. "*Hvor er han?*"

With a pained flinch, he rolled his head to the side, turning away from her.

The man was a fool if he thought her so easily put off. She

crouched down, grabbed his chin, and yanked him back to face her. *"Hvor er han?"*

He curled his lip as though she stunk. *"Hore."*

A spear embedded itself deep in the man's chest.

She twisted around and looked up to find Thorburn, his face red with rage.

"No one calls my lady love a whore."

"Since when do you speak Norwegian?" She stood and eased his hand away from the quivering shaft of the weapon.

"I dinna speak it, but an insult is plain in any tongue." With a gentle tug, he pulled her into his arms. "None of these men will speak against him. Not if they are all like this one."

"They are all like this one," she admitted quietly, even though the truth pained her. Her people had turned on her long ago. Alrek had seen to it.

With a tender kiss to the top of her head, he held her for a moment longer, then took her hand and led her up the steps.

"Where do we go?" She hurried along beside him, scrambling to maneuver the piles of stone and great wooden beams awaiting the craftsmen's use.

"Away from the field. The stench of this failure sickens me."

"This is no failure. Not a one of your men fell—did they?"

He didn't answer. Just kept striding across the bailey with the force of a charging bull. They entered the largest completed room in the keep. Workers emerged from every archway, creeping into the torchlit room. Reassured that the fighting had ended, they hurried outside, their curiosity getting the better of them.

Crude tables and benches filled the cavernous space, now empty except for them. Stone dust and rubble covered the floor, but the tables appeared to have been wiped down. Adellis recognized this as the chief gathering place, destined to be the chief's great hall where everyone would eat and claim fealty to their liege.

"Did you see their faces?" she asked. The man would have to blind to miss their relief. It had shone from them brighter than the torches. "You protected them. This is not a failure."

That won her a grudging side-eyed glance but still no smile. With a weary huff, he lowered himself to a bench and patted the place beside him. "Come. Sit with me, love. Grant me the comfort of yer company."

"Comfort?" She sat and nudged him with her shoulder. "You sound like a man already long in the tooth and short in the bed." She needed him happy. Uplifted. When his spirits flagged, hers dragged even lower.

Finally, he revealed those straight white teeth in the devilish smile she loved. "Dinna fash yerself, love. Later, I shall be more than happy to prove that ye have nay chosen an old man to walk with ye through this life."

Adellis found herself without a response. Walk with him through this life? A promising notion, but also terrifying. Did he mean what it sounded like he meant? As his smile brightened even more, she realized she sat with her mouth open but no words coming forth. "Uhm."

His deep, rumbling laugh echoed to the rafters. "Is *uhm* Norwegian for ye agree to be my wife?"

"You are a mercenary. The constable of Argyll's vast legion of *Gallóglaigh*. A man such as yourself does not marry."

"I do as I wish." He hugged an arm around her. "I have lands. Titles, even, although I canna remember all of them." He nuzzled a kiss behind her earlobe. "As I said, I do as I wish."

"Your Lord of Argyll might have something to say about that." Bitter victory soured on her tongue as his mood shifted and the sweet nuzzling ended. She hated to be right, but the proof of it shone in his face.

He cleared his throat and sat taller. "I will go to him upon our return. Ye will see."

"I fear I shall," she said softly, frowning down at the rough-hewn table beneath her hands. The Lord of Argyll would accept a Norwegian slave without blinking an eye, but a Norwegian wife for his constable? Doubtful.

"My lady?"

Adellis turned toward the soft greeting. Midst all the turmoil, she had forgotten about poor Gerdy. "I am glad to see you safe. What is it?"

The girl held out a plank bearing two steaming cups but didn't smile nor meet eyes with either of them. Instead, she stared downward, occasionally stealing furtive glances toward a doorway a few steps away. "A brew," she whispered in the same despairing tone she had used back at Alrek's camp.

"Gerdy?"

The waif made a nervous shrug, her wide eyes glistening with unshed tears. "A brew," she repeated even softer.

Thorburn gave Adellis a quizzical look, then lifted the cup. He sniffed at the liquid, wrinkled his nose, and set it back on the plank. "Thank ye, but no, lass. 'Tis ale or whisky for me. Soon as I see Hendry, he shall fetch it." A frown puckered his brow. "Have ye seen Hendry? 'Tis unlike the lad to go missing once the fighting is done."

Gerdy twitched another timid shrug, then again shot a sidling glance at a darkened arch beneath what would someday be the second-floor gallery.

Adellis followed Gerdy's focus of interest without overtly looking in that direction. She picked up the cup and pretended to sniff it, then took it to her lips. Hiding her words behind the vessel, she whispered, "Alrek is here. In the shadows. Yes?"

The girl didn't speak, just bobbed a curtsy and stared at the mixture Thorburn had rejected. She lifted the makeshift tray and offered it to him again. "A blade is held at Hendry's throat," she said, nodding at the cup as if explaining the brew. "Jarl Alrek watches. Do not drink it." She dipped her chin again, and she pressed the tray closer. "Do not drink. But for Hendry's sake, make it look as if you do."

Adellis feigned at taking another long slow sip, hiding her words again. "How should I act to show the poisoning?"

Gerdy forced a smile and lifted the tray to accept both the

drinking bowls as though they were empty. "Cough. Thrash. Go still." She made another curtsy and shuffled off toward a doorway on the other side of the room.

"He is mine," Adellis whispered against Thorburn's cheek as she rose from the bench.

With her in his embrace and his hand at her nape, he kissed her, nibbling his words across her mouth as if teasing the kiss. "*Ours,* m'love. Ye willna go alone, ye ken?"

She answered with a seductive smile, playing the part her brother would expect. Hooking her hand in his, she led Thorburn toward the archway as though seeking privacy. Once within a full stride of the doorway, he grabbed hold of his throat, coughing and choking as he first dropped to his knees, then fell across the floor.

Adellis did the same, clutching at her chest, coughing as though strangling. All the while, she kept the arch within view. When Alrek failed to show, she remained motionless, keeping her eyes open to slits.

Thorburn kept flailing about until she toyed with the notion of feigning one more seizure so she could kick him. The man was going to spoil their trap. He needed to stop overplaying the part. With a groan that made her want to roll her eyes, her Scottish bear at long last lay in a motionless heap.

A scrabbling across the flagstones, like the scratching of a rat, reached her ears. It was a rat, all right. Alrek was most certainly a vile rodent with a vicious bite. It took all her patience to remain still as the footsteps drew closer.

"Your master is not so mighty now." Alrek shoved Hendry to his knees, blocking her view of Thorburn. "No *Gallóglaigh* can best a pure Viking."

With the devil's back to her, now was her chance. She sprang upward and plunged her dagger up into Alrek's back, aiming for a kidney. Burying it to the hilt, she twisted as she yelled, "Roll away, Hendry!"

The bound and gagged knave flailed over to the side.

Thorburn surged upward and buried his blade in Alrek's stomach.

Alrek sputtered and choked out garbled words. Blood streamed from his mouth as he went to his knees.

"No Valhalla for you, my brother." She kicked him to the floor and took hold of his hair, forcing him to look at her. "Hell awaits you. I hope you enjoy it."

"I will see you there, bitch," he wheezed with a futile attempt to bat her away.

Thorburn grabbed hold of the man's head and twisted with a hard jerk, filling the chamber with a deadly crackling.

Alrek went limp, and Thorburn let him drop to the floor.

"I was not done," she sobbed, frustrated at a sudden trembling she couldn't seem to stop. Why had he done that? She wanted to torture Alrek, make him pay for all the pain he had caused.

"Aye, ye are plenty done, m'love." Ever so gently, he took her into his arms and held her. "Ye ended it. Now, let it go, and give it no more power over ye."

The harder she shook, the more she realized Thorburn spoke the truth. Alrek would only be truly dead if she cast away the past and never let it touch her again. She sagged into his chest and sobbed, the first cleansing tears she had ever cried.

CHAPTER NINE

EYES CLOSED, SHE faced the wind, enjoying its brisk touch and briny taste. Rough waters rocked the ship, and she loved it. Every wave hitting the hull swayed Thorburn against her backside, reminding her of when he had bent her over during their first night of enjoying each other. Her heart raced at the memory of the delicious pounding, causing her to hitch in a deep breath. His arms tightened around her waist, and he nibbled kisses along her neck, making her need him even more.

"Surely, we could find a quiet corner." She spun in his embrace so the movement of the ship could shove him against her front.

"'Tis a fine-sized birlinn, but it isna known for privacy." He settled her back against the railing and planted his hands on either side of her. With the crash of the next swell, he notched himself into her curves and emitted a low, rumbling groan. "But we will make landfall first. Just ahead, in fact. Then we shall find a quiet corner."

"A full sail and rowers for such a short crossing?" She grazed the tip of her tongue along his throat, tracing the corded ridges of his tensed muscles. He wanted her as much as she wanted him. Good. They had indulged in each other before leaving Duart, but that had been hours ago. She needed him again. "Your men must sense our urgency."

"How can they not?" He cast a sideways glance over his

shoulder and grinned. "We're dead in their sights."

"Port ho! Boat yer oars and ready the lines!"

"Thank God," he rasped as he nipped her earlobe.

She smiled, turning to see the much-anticipated port. The imposing sight made her swallow hard. "Is that Dunstaffnage?"

"Aye." Stretching around to look her in the eyes, he frowned. "What is it, love? I hear worry in yer voice."

She dreaded standing in front of the Lord of Argyll. Alexander MacDougall. Known for his ferocity and refusal to bend. And thanks to her vile brother, the man despised all Northmen. With a seductiveness she almost had to force, she wiggled back against Thorburn and brushed aside his words. "I had hoped we could enjoy each other, my love. Before we faced your liege."

"We will," he promised, gently nipping at her ear again. He gave her bottom a reassuring squeeze. "This early in the day, the MacDougall will most likely be on a hunt or one of his adventures. He isna the sort of man who lounges about waiting to be entertained. We shall meet with him tonight just before the feast."

That eased her some, even though she realized she merely delayed the inevitable. She kept her gaze locked on the formidable stronghold looming up ahead. Its weathered walls sprouted from a stony outcrop, making the fortress appear as though it had risen from the earth's very bowels. The windows and arrow slits scowled at her. Bellowed their accusations that she did not belong on the hallowed ground of Scotland.

As they moored, Thorburn swept her up into his arms, stepped out onto the pier, and carried her to the worn path leading from the shoreline to the castle. As he set her feet to the ground, he nodded toward a fork up ahead in the walkway. "To the left leads to the chapel." His devilish smile did not suggest piety.

"The chapel?"

"Aye," he said, seduction gleaming in his eyes. "Quiet corners there, ye ken?"

She had been called a *hore* or whore many times because of her robust enjoyment of lovers, but not once had she ever desecrated a holy place with what everyone called her low morals. "A house of God is not a *quiet corner* meant for what we intend."

"Aye, m'love, but what about the woodlands and secluded benches at the edge of the kirkyard?"

"The weather *is* very fine today." A good hard pleasuring would most definitely work out the tensed knots in her shoulders. Before she started down the path, he swept her up into his arms again.

"Allow me, m'lady."

"I am going to allow you." She wrapped an arm around his neck and outlined his ear with the tip of her tongue. "As many times as you wish." She didn't speak her fear that this might be their last joining. After all, the Lord of Argyll could very well banish her from their midst, and her Scottish bear would have no choice but to bid her farewell. No man would step away from his ancestry. From all he had worked for. And she would never demand such a sacrifice from Thorburn. "Find us a place, my love. I need you to take me."

He strode faster down the path, just as she knew he would.

"Here." He came to a stop but didn't set her down. "Will this do, m'love?"

The fern-covered wood shading the chapel promised seclusion. The coolness of its shadows offered respite from the heat certain to ignite between them. Tender moss, greener than the finest emerald, covered the exposed roots of the trees, lending its softness as a cushion for their bodies. The wind rustling in the leaves overhead gave her the gentling she needed to set her worries aside and think of nothing but this wondrous man holding her.

"This will most definitely do," she said, nuzzling the tender warm flesh behind his ear.

He lowered her feet to the ground, then claimed her with a

kiss that revealed his need matched her own. His hands raced across her, tugging at her clothes with a frustrated urgency that filled her with both longing and amusement. Her laughter bubbled between them, breaking their fiery connection. With an apologetic squeeze of his arm, she took a step back. "Let me."

Thankfully, back at Duart, a pair of kindly village women had provided her with attire more appropriate for a meeting with the Lord of Argyll. However, while the linen shift, woolen kirtle, and belted surcoat might be more suitable, the garments created a more challenging barrier between herself and Thorburn. Especially when they both longed for the pleasure of each other's complete nakedness—not merely a tossing up of her skirts for the relief of a quick tumble.

She unbelted, untied, and peeled off the layers, shook them out, and draped them over a low-hanging limb. When she turned and discovered Thorburn still fully clothed, she gave him a stern tip of her head. "Are you waiting for Hendry to come and undress you?"

He swallowed hard and licked his lips. "Nay, lass." He hurried to kick off his boots, then stepped closer, yanking his tunic off over his head and tossing it aside. "'Tis yer beauty, m'love. It mesmerizes me." His touch slid across her, leaving a burning trail in its wake. It was now her turn to swallow hard.

"And now yer trews, my love," she said ever so softly, undoing each button of the breeks with teasing slowness.

"Aye," he rasped, staring down at her hands. "Ye're doing quite nicely, love. Please dinna stop now."

Trews undone, she slipped her hands inside. She cupped his buttocks, then skimmed them down his corded muscles, shoving the garment to the ground. Running her hands back up his legs, she paused midway and took him in her mouth.

"God's beard," he groaned, rising to the balls of his feet. He tangled his fingers in her hair, dislodging her circlet and mangling the simple braid she had carefully plaited. Unintelligible words escaped him in another rumbling groan as she sucked harder.

One hand locked on his buttock, the other cradling his tight bollocks, she treated the length of him with another long slow lick, then smiled up at him. "So, this pleases you then?"

He grabbed hold of her shoulders and set her away. "Ye have no idea, lass, but, God help me, ye must stop. I'll nay have ye spill me before I've enjoyed a wee tasting myself." Before she could argue, he scooped her up, carried her to an inviting cradle of moss, and stretched her out beneath him. With a glint in his eyes that made her shudder, he eased her knees farther apart and softy blew, fanning her wanting into a raging blaze.

His short beard tickled up and down her inner thighs, making her ache in anticipation. "You are too slow, my love." She rose and took hold of his head, arched to meet him, and guided his mouth downward. Then she held on tight, releasing herself to his mouth. His mastery layered the wondrous sensations until she bucked and shrieked.

He lifted his head and smiled. "Now," he rumbled, plunging in deep as he settled on top of her. His face glistened with the wetness of her pleasure. Slow and steady, he slid out, then drove back in, all the while keeping his gaze locked with hers.

"Harder," she ordered, unable to bear the teasing any longer. She needed him. Hard. Fast. Furious.

"As ye wish." He gave himself over to pounding, unleashing the raw fury she needed.

She raked her nails down his back and arched to meet him thrust for thrust, slamming her body into his until his hoarse guttural roars drowned out her cries. He collapsed atop her, and she held on tight, suddenly beset with the fear that this could be the last time she would love this man. The terrible thought forced a hitching sob from her lips before she could bite it back.

"Forgive me, love," he breathed, gasping to catch his breath as he propped himself off her. "I didna mean to crush ye, dear one." He pressed his forehead to hers, then kissed the tip of her nose. "I love ye, Adellis. God help ye, woman, ye've made me love ye with a fierceness I canna explain."

"Do not say that," she whispered, clutching him back down atop her. She shut her eyes tight against the thought of a life without him. "Please."

He pushed himself up again and frowned down at her. "Why do ye say that?" His eyes flexed into tighter slits the longer she took to reply. "Adellis?"

"Because we will be—"

"Constable? Uhm, m'lord?" Hendry's hesitant call spared her from having to speak the doom looming over them.

"I will kill him," Thorburn promised through clenched teeth. He lifted his head higher and turned toward the call. "Ye value yer life verra little, Hendry!"

"Forgive me, m'lord, but Himself has ordered ye fetched."

The center of her chest ached, as though a gaping hole had been punched through it. Their time was done. With a gentle push, she forced out the words she didn't want to say. "We must go to him, my love. Now."

⇥⇥⇥✳⇤⇤⇤

HER HAND ON his arm was cold as the sea in the dead of winter. Thorburn covered it with his, willing her to believe all would be well. No hint of color brightened her fair cheeks. He feared if he didn't hold tight to her, she would faint dead away. Halting just outside the entry hall, he slid a finger beneath her chin and gently forced her to meet his gaze. "Where is my warrior queen?" he whispered.

"She has left me, my bear. She cannot brave the pain I carry."

"There will be no pain. I swear it."

"Thor!" The summons shook through the keep like a roared battle cry.

With a twisting jerk, she shirked away from his touch and stepped through the doorway without him. Unsmiling. Proud. Regal. She strode up the center aisle of the great hall and came to a halt within a few feet in front of the MacDougall and his wife. After a graceful curtsy, she lowered her gaze and kept it locked on the floor. "My liege, I am Adellis Bjørnsdóttir."

Thorburn strode across the length of the large gathering room as though it spanned less than the width of his palm. With a proud squaring of his shoulders, he took his place at Adellis's side. After a respectful nod, he thumped a fist to his chest. "M'lord."

Ruddy hair, flaming cheeks, and a fierce temper to match, Alexander MacDougall, Lord of Argyll, tightened his massive hands on the carved arms of his chair. "Instead of reporting to yer chief, ye choose to bed yer Norwegian whore among the trees shading my chapel?"

Protective rage flared hot and hard at the insult. "She is not a Norwegian whore," Thorburn growled, not bothering to veil the threat dripping from his words. He took Adellis's hand and placed it on his forearm. "She is my wife."

The MacDougall's face flared even redder. His wife reached across the narrow space between their chairs and rested her hand on his arm. The fair Lady Christiana had always been the soothing tonic to the chief's volatile temper.

"Yer knave reported ye used my resources to fetch this one ye call yer *wife* from that bastard brother of hers." The MacDougall started to rise, but his wife's grip on his arm must have tightened because he turned and looked at her instead. After the merest dip of her head, he settled back in his chair with an irritated snort. "Since when do ye waste my men and supplies?" His furious scowl shifted to Adellis's bowed head. "And for a Norwegian, at that. One, who I might add, I sent ye to oust from Mull?"

"My knave?" Thorburn repeated, resisting the urge to call the MacDougall a liar. While the information was true, neither Hendry nor Tasgall would ever repeat the details of a campaign without express permission. Who was this knave who had gone to the chieftain behind his back?

"Get him in here," the MacDougall ordered.

The guard beside the dais disappeared. After a moment, he

returned with the knave in tow.

Thorburn curled his fingers until his knuckles popped. Hendry was right. Wylie Dowall was indeed a devious wee shite who would do anything to lift himself up in the world. What the conniving little bastard didn't realize was the MacDougall never tolerated a traitor—even a traitor who fed him information. Such a person could never be trusted. If they turned on one, they would turn on all.

"All I reported was true," Wylie said, defiance ringing in his sniveling whine. When his focus shifted to the other side of the room, his eyes flared wide, and he paled.

Thorburn turned to see what had triggered the coward's reaction. Tasgall and Hendry stood side by side, looking ready to tear Wylie to shreds. Good. He would leave them to it when this was all said and done.

"Well?" The MacDougall glare had settled back on him.

"It is all true." Thorburn threw out his chest and widened his stance. "And once recovered, my lady love helped us discover her brother's plans, fought at our sides, and struck the first blow in the killing of him."

"And I would kill him again if given the chance." For the first time since introducing herself, Adellis lifted her head. "He was a crazed fool, my lord. I am sorry for all he cost you."

Lady Christiana twitched in her seat, then tugged on the MacDougall's arm until he leaned close enough for her to whisper in his ear. Once she finished speaking, he stared at her. After a pointed look and a single nod, she released her hold on him and folded her hands in her lap.

Nostrils flaring, the MacDougall huffed out a defeated snort. His face calmed to a lighter shade of red as he settled back in his seat and stroked his beard. "Ye have lands and titles," he said. "All granted by me. I could just as easily take it all away, ye ken?"

"Aye." Thorburn couldn't resist a smirk. "And my brothers and I could as easily leave ye. Taking our might and a damned good lot of yer men with us." To defy the man would mean having to leave Scotland. The MacDougall had King Alexander's ear and would use it without hesitation. Or perhaps not. With the battle prowess he and his brothers possessed, they were known far and wide. Another clan would take them in merely to boast they had won away the Lord of Argyll's mighty *Gallóglaigh*. Thorburn knew more than just his brothers would leave with him as well. From the frustration knotting the MacDougall's bushy brows, the man knew it, too.

"I dinna tolerate anyone using *my* resources to benefit themselves," the MacDougall said. "Even if it ends in the results I desire." He stabbed a finger in the air. "Ye ken that well enough, Thor, and yet ye did it, anyway."

"Aye, I did." Thorburn slid his arm back beneath Adellis's hand and presented her as if she were his queen. "And I would do it again. I love this woman and will do anything to keep her safe."

"This conversation is going in naught but circles," Lady Christiana interrupted. With a calm, unreadable expression, she rested her gaze first on Adellis then slid it to Thorburn. "Sentence them."

The MacDougall slowly rose. His height rivaled that of Thorburn's, but his build was far less muscular. With a fierce scowl, he snapped his fingers at the nearby guard. "Fetch the scribe."

Adellis's fingers dug into his arm, but she didn't falter, just stared straight ahead at the MacDougall and his wife.

Pride swelled Thorburn's chest. God had saddled him with a rare woman, indeed. "It will be well with us, m'love," he whispered. "I swear to make it so."

The Lord of Argyll's eyes narrowed. "What say ye?"

"I swore to my lady love that all would be well." He allowed his own eyes to narrow into a look the MacDougall couldn't fail to read. "And it will be. One way or another."

A tiny man, arms full of ledgers and stacks of parchment, hurried into the room. He dumped the load on a small table nearby, pulled an inkwell from his pocket, and removed the quill from behind his ear. "Ye summoned me, m'lord?"

"Aye," the MacDougall said as he folded his massive arms

over this chest. "Take this down."

The mousie scribe crouched over the papers with quill in hand, looking ready to pounce.

"Ye disobeyed yer lord and liege, leaving me no recourse, Constable Thorburn MacDougall." The man glared down his long nose like the fiercest god about to wreak destruction.

Adellis's nails dug deeper into his arm. As subtly as possible, he disengaged the wee scratching fury and took her hand in his. He stood taller. "Aye? Get on with it then." Lord MacDougall had always been a long-winded bastard that took forever to get to the point.

The man snorted out a growl, glanced back at Lady Christiana, then cleared his throat. "I sentence ye to a life of servitude."

"Servitude?" Thorburn didn't know whether to draw his sword and fight their way out of the room or stay long enough to hear more. The man hadn't called for more guards. Surely, he didn't think the one guard and himself could handle the job.

"Aye. Servitude," the chieftain repeated, then held out a hand for his wife to stand at his side. "Ye call that woman yer wife, but I willna allow such an irregular marriage in my lands. One as easy to cast aside as it is to make. Nay, man. I sentence ye to a formal legal marriage recorded in the church and sent to Edinburgh. Ye will stand before the priest when we're done here." He gave a solemn nod. "May God have mercy on yer souls."

"Does he jest?" Adellis whispered.

"Nay, lass." Thorburn gave Lady Christiana a thankful bow and added a grin as he gave the MacDougall a slight nod.

"Aye, ye grin now, but ye'll learn soon the way of things." The Lord of Argyll pecked a quick kiss to his wife's cheek. "To the priest now. My lady and I shall be yer witnesses."

Turning Adellis to face him, Thorburn held both her hands in his. He struggled to find the words to convey all he felt. "I love ye, Adellis. And I shall be saying so all the rest of my days, so ye best get used to it, ye ken?"

"Yes, my Scottish bear." She squeezed his hands and smiled. "I love you, too."

EPILOGUE

Dunthoradelle Castle
Argyll, Scotland
Gallóglaigh Training Camp
September 1275

As THORBURN SLOWLY strolled back and forth atop the wall overlooking the northern practice grounds, the stairwell tunnel accessing the western end of the walkway echoed with a sneeze as loud as the blast of a horn. He turned toward it and waited for the owner of the horrendous noise to appear.

Ross limped into view with one eye swollen shut, both nostrils crusty with dried blood, and the front of his tunic torn and splattered with more of the same. His split bottom lip had fattened to three times its normal size.

"Damn, brother. Ye look worse than ye did after Ireland." Thorburn grinned, ready for what he felt certain would be excellent entertainment on this fine crisp morning.

Ross shielded the eye that remained open and scowled. "Her feckin' husband came home early."

Thorburn chuckled and shook his head. "Ye never learn." He eyed his brother again. "And from the looks of it, ye didna defend our prowess in battle all that well. Pray tell me her husband looks worse than yerself."

"I'd like to see ye best Lachren Martmullen." Ross sneezed again, wincing as he dabbed his sleeve to his nose. "It's bleeding again. I think he broke it."

"Ye always sneeze when yer nose is broken." Thorburn shook his head, then meandered farther down the walkway to get a closer look at the new group of potential archers. The name his brother had uttered replayed with a vengeance. He shot an incredulous frown back at Ross. "Lachren Martmullen? Ye're lucky ye made it out alive." Brawnier than all three of the MacDougall brothers put together, the infamous Lachren might only have one good eye, but the beast of a man still cleared out his pub single-handedly—even when it was filled with mighty *Gallóglaigh*. "Was she worth it?"

Ross shrugged while testing to see if one of his teeth would wiggle. "I dinna ken for sure. We hadna got good and started." He perked up and forgot about checking for missing teeth. "Is that Adellis? And wee Mathan?"

Mathan Beag. Adellis had insisted on naming their son *little bear.* Thorburn swelled with pride. "Aye. Her skill with the longbow has helped our archers tenfold. Her training saved the ones we sent to Burgundy."

Clad in her Norwegian armor Tasgall had repaired, she marched up and down the line with six-month-old Mathan harnessed to her chest. Every time his mother shouted an order, the feisty bairn cut loose with a loud stream of babbling that only he understood. Then he batted both tiny fists as if threatening his mother's students with their lives. Thorburn loved it. Aye, this was worth settling down and overseeing training rather than trotting off to war whenever the Lord of Argyll got the itch for more land.

"Those who can, do. Those who canna do—teach it, aye?" Ross added a brotherly wink to the ribbing, then winced and gingerly touched the area around his eye. "Is this one swelling, too?"

"It will be when I'm done with ye," Thorburn said but didn't mean it. Well, perhaps he meant it a wee bit. "I am still constable. Shall I order ye to oversee delivery of the barrels due us from

Lachren's pub?"

"I said it in jest. Ye should ken that well enough." Ross flipped a hand in Adellis's direction. "Wave her up here, aye? I've no' seen my fine nephew in well over a month." Even with his swollen lip, he managed a grin. "I'm sure he missed his favorite uncle since Valan's gone to Skye." Suddenly serious, he added, "He is well, aye? I'd hate to be stuck with just yerself as a brother."

"He is well." Thorburn caught Adellis's eye and motioned for her to join them. "We received word yesterday."

"Good. I hadna heard since I made landfall." The split in his lip bled anew as his smile widened. He lifted a hand, then bowed at Adellis and Mathan emerging from the east stairwell.

"Have you learned nothing?" Adellis spared him no sympathy. With a finger held firmly in each of her son's chubby fists, she tipped her head forward and murmured against his flaxen hair. "Never behave like Uncle Ross, my son."

The baby crowed with a happy chortling and kicked his feet, bouncing in the leather harness Tasgall had fashioned to permit his mother to tote him everywhere but keep her hands free.

"For shame, good sister. How do ye ken I didna come straight here from battle?"

"The mark on your neck is in the shape of a woman's mouth." She arched a brow. "Or did an eel latch hold of you during your voyage?"

"Ye willna best her, brother." Thorburn smiled at his wife and son. "Neither her nor my wee Mathan."

"M'lord!" A young lad known to be a runner for the Lord of Argyll sprinted toward them.

Thorburn tensed. When Adellis first got with child, he had made it clear that he would not leave Dunthoradelle Castle for any more campaigns unless ordered to do so by King Alexander himself. He would train the mighty *Gallóglaigh* and forge them into warriors of the strongest steel, but his own warring days had ended. But lieges were known to decide otherwise, no matter whose lives they shattered. He accepted the parchment from the messenger, clenching his teeth at the Lord of Argyll's insignia in the blood-red wax seal. He broke the wax, popped open the flap, then blew out a breath of relief.

"What is it?" Adellis whispered, worry drawing her closer.

"A summons." He held it out to his brother. "For Ross."

Ross snatched hold of the paper and scanned the flowery scrawl. "I already turned over the prisoners and reported the details of the campaign. What more does he need?"

"That is his own hand," Thorburn said, nodding toward the note. "He doesna sound…angry."

"I know," Ross said. "That's what worries me." As if Thorburn and Adellis didn't exist, Ross turned and slowly limped back toward the stairwell.

"What do you think it is?" Adellis asked, her gaze locked on her brother-in-law's back.

"It mentioned a rare reward for a task well done." Thorburn lifted his son out of the harness and held him in one arm while curling the other around his lady love and pulling her close. "And with the MacDougall, rewards are always double-edged blades."

Adellis snuggled tighter against him and smiled. "It might be selfish, but I'm more than a little glad my reward is still safe here in my arms."

Thorburn bent his head for a sweet kiss, pausing only long enough to say, "I'm glad ye're selfish, m'love. Because I am, too."

About the Author

If you enjoyed A SCOT OF HER OWN, please consider leaving a review on the site where you purchased your copy, or a reader site such as Goodreads, or BookBub.

If you'd like to receive my newsletter, here's the link to sign up:
maevegreyson.com/contact.html#newsletter

I love to hear from readers! Drop me a line at:
maeve@maevegreyson.com

Or visit me on Facebook:
facebook.com/AuthorMaeveGreyson

I'm also on Instagram:
maevegreyson

My website:
https://maevegreyson.com

Feel free to ask questions or leave some Reader Buzz on:
bingebooks.com/author/maeve-greyson

Follow me on these sites to get notifications about new releases, sales, and special deals:

BookBub:
bookbub.com/authors/maeve-greyson

Many thanks, and may your life always be filled with good books!
Maeve